A CUPPA, A NATTER & HIDDEN GEMS

MARIE CLAIRE – MY LIFE STORY

BY VERA LINDA MELLOR

ABOUT THE AUTHOR

I, Vera L Mellor have resided in High Peak, North Derbyshire for 35 years. This wonderful area with its beautiful scenery, ideal for outdoor pursuits and teeming with wildlife, has inspired me to write three books on interesting country walks. In addition to creative writing, my main hobbies are local history, country walking, nature, travel, music, local radio, country and disco dancing.

However, when a local community centre advertised Wednesday Coffee Mornings, inviting anyone with spare time who enjoys these type of daytime social activities to "join us for a cuppa and natter – all welcome", I was struck with idea for a novel. It's set in a small town community centre where one of its keen members shares her interesting life story with several other regulars. This has an impact on the centre which no one could have ever predicted.

Anyway I do like a challenge and so this is my first foray into the realm of fiction. I hope my readers will enjoy this experience.

COPYRIGHT STATEMENT & PUBLISHER'S DETAILS

ISBN 978-0-9551631-2-8

Titles of Sections within
Marie–Claire, My Life Story

For my family and my many good friends in High Peak, North Derbyshire. I also include my more far-flung friends who have also been supportive in my various enterprises.

A Cuppa, a Natter & Hidden Gems

This story begins in a fictitious small market town in High Peak, North Derbyshire, Torr Brookdale and most of the action takes place in the local community centre where Gloria Redfern is the co-ordinator of social activities for the 55+ age group at the centre. Gloria is in her late fifties, with a lively, outgoing personality, good sense of humour and a warm, caring nature so is ideal for this post.

PROLOGUE

What a night it had been but not one to be remembered for the best of reasons. However, Gloria Redfern, along with her husband Joe, was usually inclined to be positive and optimistic even when either bad news or negative, depressing situations prevailed. Their Christian faith never failed to give them hope and peace of mind in the long run. This spirit was much needed in view of the news that she and her fellow committee members received this evening.

As she drove back from Torr Brookdale Community Centre to her home in the village of Badgers' Rise about 2 miles down the road, Gloria, in common with all who attended the council meeting, was still reeling from the shock of receiving word from the North West Derbyshire Community Fund, informing the centre's manager, staff and volunteers that their annual grant would be stopped, being no longer available for them in the new financial year. There was seven months to go before this funding source would end but would this be sufficient notice in which to find alternative financial support to replace it? After all the reports from the centre's manager secretary, treasurer, social activities department, economies were earnestly discussed as were possible alternative sources of finance. The overall picture didn't look too hopeful but local businesses or some relevant charitable trust seemed to be their best bet.

Gloria's mind was so pre-occupied with this problem that she nearly missed the turning for the lane leading up to Badger's Rise, a picturesque hamlet where they lived. "Oh botheration, pull yourself together girl," Gloria muttered to herself. "Take it to the top.! Write to the Prime Minister1"

Gloria heaved a sigh of relief as she entered their driveway. Home at last! The meeting had, of course, been prolonged because of the serious problem which had arisen. Thank goodness I can discuss this with Joe.

His level-headed, commonsense approach to any problem arising and his reassuring presence plus a wry sense of humour was a godsend in this situation. Joe would have been present at the meeting as he was a regular helper at the Boy's Brigade who met at the centre on Friday nights but tonight's meeting clashed with his meeting of the Torr Brookdale Railway Users Association of which he was a keen member. Railways were always a passion of Joe's and a source of endless interest and fascination. Every year without fail and despite his job as a self-employed joiner he spent between a week to ten days as a volunteer on steam heritage railways in various parts of the country. He ardently supported any campaign to protect existing local rail services or any proposal to re-open any railway in the area which had been axed by Dr Beeching during the late 1960's closures.

In their cosy lounge Gloria & Joe discussed their experiences at their respective meetings. Joe's rail users meeting was interesting as they were discussing possible reasons for delay in building a tram link between Stockport and Manchester Piccadilly Station as there appeared to be much progress made on the north side of Manchester . Details about contacting Northern Rail also received considerable attention. However Joe's meeting ended earlier than Gloria's so he made them both a mug of hot chocolate just in time for Gloria coming home. "Thanks Joe, this is just what I need so I can relax after what's been a rather challenging meeting!"

"Aye I know what it's like with you women at any meeting. Put most politicians in the shade when there's a long-winded natter involved," Joe replied in a light, amused tone.

"Oh, you men have some room to talk," protested Gloria in mock indignation, giving Joe a thump with the newspaper.

"What about when you and Jeff get together for a chinwag about railways and football. It's at least a 2 hour job then!"

Jeff Miller was their neighbour and, together with his wife Diane, both couples were on friendly terms, sharing similar interests but they only met up occasionally due to the Millers' work and family commitments which had increased of late because of their becoming grandparents for the first time.

"So your meeting turned out to be an urgent discussion tonight. Did you all get some unwelcome news?"

"You can say that again! Our NWD Community Fund will be withdrawn in seven months' time. As you know our council funding only covers essential costs so we'll need to make some economies and seek replacement finance elsewhere. We'll really have to put our thinking caps on to find imaginative ways to fund raise within Torr Brookdale and district."

"Yes, you'll need to raise enough to apply for a National Lottery Grant so that they'll know you mean business and your finance plan isn't a nine day wonder. It's a bit much though being as our centre's such an all round success in our community. Us working closely with the local churches to provide quality entertainment and activities for the teenagers is a big help in keeping them off the streets and out of the clutches of drug dealers who seem to be around everywhere these days" sympathized Joe. "Still there's enough local firms and companies around town which seem to keep going. No rumours of any of 'em likely to go bust in the near future. Surely some of them could cough up some significant amounts of cash now and then. By the way, I hope the gloom and doom drama queen didn't lay it on with a trowel too heavily on hearing this bad news."

Joe was referring to Beryl Greenfield, the centre's efficient but serious minded and overly cautious secretary, prone to pessimism.

"Oh, our Beryl doubtless would predict bankruptcy and closure" Gloria replied ruefully. "Her reaction fortunately wasn't too discouraging. She was right about one thing though. Other than Mondays when we're closed anyway, one obvious economy would be to close the centre for one other additional day. However it would be a heck of a job deciding which day to choose that would cause the least inconvenience to our users and staff. I'll suggest Sunday as that's a day when most people, prefer to do other things, some going to church or visiting or just relaxing. Although the bar's open on Sunday afternoons, other than a one off special event, we don't appear to have many folk turning up then. We all decided to hold a coffee morning most Saturdays, advertise our club as a social venue for special occasions and celebrations more widely and frequently than before, stage film shows on our full screen at least once per month and hold a mega table-top sale with tombola, raffle tickets, fun competitions, children's entertainment such as face painting, a puppet shows, etc on four Saturdays during the year. All this should hopefully generate extra income to keep our centre solvent."

"It looks like you've already got the situation under control" Joe remarked. "Anyway, Bob the financial wizard, from what I've heard, seems to have some influential contacts in this area and he certainly has some flair and imagination for an accountant. They're usually rather staid, overly cautious, boring sort of guys. Not our Bob though!"

Joe was referring to the centre's treasurer, a colourful character named Robert Aaron Silverwaters, a Jewish gentlemen from Manchester where he'd previously ran a computer training company, prospered financially through the business, sold it at a profit now he was in his fifties and, once he'd lived in Torr Brookdale for eight years, applied for and successfully secured the post of treasurer. His financial competence, business flair and pleasant, confident personality won over his interviewers, the committee that day. Robert still had commercial contacts whereby items for the centre could be purchased more cheaply than through the usual sources. He had a personality quirk which staff and volunteers alike found amusing as long as they weren't working too closely with him over a long period of time. He often sang to himself, usually a pop classic, jazz, country & western or operetta tune, making a sound like a cross between a whistle and a hum rather like a cat's purr. Sometimes it became more high pitched when he "sang" a particularly lively tune. "It's a wonder he can concentrate on his work" Gloria sometimes thought. However it never adversely affected his work so not even fussy Beryl minded.

"Anyway", Joe continued. "I'm sure our Bob can help to save this situation from disaster. A good dose of positive thinking is what's needed here. I'm fairly certain you may think of this yourself Glo but here's a suggestion from me. Perhaps our regular users, especially those who take part in several different social activities, might come up with some new suggestions, some we've not yet considered.

After all, we've members of all ages so it would be silly and short-sighted as well as unfair to underestimate their possible contribution towards keeping our centre thriving."

"Joe, you've hit the nail on the head! "Don't know what I'd do without you." Gloria gave him a hug. "As regards my senior citizens group, the famous four spring to mind immediately as likely participants."

"Oh there's four of them now is there?" asked Joe. As far as I'm aware there were just the three ladies."

"Well they've been recently joined by a fourth member, Marie Claire, originally from Belgium who was a war bride when a young woman. Her country was one of those liberated from Nazi occupation during World War 2. She married a British serviceman. From all reports she's a very lively, interesting person, still leading an active life despite being close on eighty-two years old, considerably older than the other three. Marie is a real inspiration to younger pensioners who might dread the thought of inactivity, ill health, disability or loneliness in their later years."

A trio of the community centre's regulars, Rosemary, Freda and Doreen, aged between 61 and 68, were the life and soul of their group, making the most of their retirement years. Rosemary, at 61 the youngest of the three was still leading a single life after being divorced many years previous. Freda, widowed for several years, had never found anyone else to replace the love of her life, Clive, to whom she'd been happily married for almost 35 years until his untimely, sudden death from heart failure. Doreen, also widowed some 10 years previous, had recently married for the second time. Her new husband, Bill and his friend Harry occasionally went out together with the others on outings and often joined them for social evenings at the centre as well.

Both Gloria and Joe had no doubts that their enthusiastic, public-spirited community would rise to the occasion when it came to suggestions and practical support for fund-raising activities.

"Anyway, we're contacting High Peak Radio tomorrow. One of their reporters might interview at least one of our staff members. That would be a very good idea as we need all the publicity we can get."

"The best idea for now will be to turn in for our beauty's sleep," Joe replied. "I need to make an early start tomorrow on that big job over at Foxlow Green. Lucky to have the opportunity of such a lucrative contract in such a quiet little hole as Foxlow Green."

Foxlow Green was a nearby village after Torr Brookdale, along the busy Transpeak road which stretched from Manchester to Nottingham, straddling the Peak District and South Derbyshire. It was a tiny village but nevertheless had a rail station, two friendly country pubs, a general store with a post office attached, a primary school, a church and village hall on its outskirts and two small industrial estates on opposite sides of its centre. Foxlow Green offered country walks, amid beautiful scenery, both on the moors above the village and below, along the banks of the Peak Forest Canal which ran alongside the railway line. The village green, which gave the place its name, was tucked away, halfway up a winding, hilly lane, several yards up from a small Continental restaurant adjoining the main road.

"Foxlow's folk 'ud give you quiet little hole if they heard you," Gloria chuckled. "On completion of your super contract are we to expect holidays in Bali, Mauritius and Palm Springs from now on and definitely Orlando, Florida for Mark, Sue, Rod and Mandy plus our grand kids, in fact all our tribe? Apart, of course, from saving our community centre in the same way as in the "Secret Millionaire" off the telly?"

"Hey, steady on! Will Blackpool Pleasure Beach or a picnic at Buxton's Grin Low Park do?" teased Joe.

"Talk about an unromantic, stick-in-the-mud Brit!" Must reach for the stars sometime you know. Anyway, to finish the subject of our centre for now, I don't think the situation is as grim as we imagine. For a start, we've two virtual geniuses in our manager Martin and Bob, our treasurer, both of whom are skilled in wording funding applications effectively. They'd also have a pretty clear idea which grants might be available."

"I'm sure you're right about that," agreed Joe . "Let's sleep on it for the time being."

"Oh, botheration! Forgot to mention a very important aspect of this business. Reverend Norman is a great believer in the power of prayer. As long as it's not self centred all the time. Usually has a story about individual instance of prayers being answered and problems solved just when everything seemed hopeless. We're supposed to be practicing Christians so prayer should be a first port of call in adverse situations."

"Reverend Norman would probably like to know when we've stopped practicing our faith and are now fully qualified in it," Joe replied cheerfully.

"Well, no one could accuse you of taking life too seriously," laughed Gloria. "Anyway, our vicar was present at tonight's meeting so I'm sure he'll be thinking about this problem, and help us towards it's solution."

Norman Redesdale was Torr Brookdale's progressive new vicar who was a lively, friendly personality who was very popular with his congregation.

"I'm sure he'd back us up with our prayers. Who better to do so? Anyway we should turn in now or at this rate we'll have it three in the morning."

The next few days in Torr Brookdale were of frenetic, bustling activity with every public-spirited person in town thinking up fund raising ideas, contacting local businesses, the local council and, indeed, any establishments and individuals possessing some power or influence to rally round in the centre's our of need. The local press were on the scene during social and sporting activities taking place at the centre in order to interview a variety of users in all age groups. In Gloria's sewing and handicraft circle for over 60's, the famous four inclusive of their new friend Marie, came up with interesting ideas which they enthusiastically put to Gloria.

"We're as excited as kids invited to a special birthday party," said Freda gleefully. "To start with, my nephew, on surfing the internet recently, found a bargain on Ebay, beautiful, high quality silk in a great variety of colours, patterned or plain, all the way from America. Certainly cheaper to buy than in this country.

We can now make some lovely evening bags, purses and cushion covers!"

"And some free publicity for Ebay!" Gloria replied in a teasing tone. "Anyway you can also do some of your silk painting, Rosemary, Freda can obtain some more silk from the same source."

"My word, we'll be busy this autumn. Our stall should raise a bumper profit for our centre at Christmas."

"I should save a few for Christmas presents for family members, friends, etc," Gloria advised. "Nevertheless I do admire your spirit and loyalty to our community."

"And now for my brainwave idea," said Marie Claire, speaking in the same eager tones. She always spoke almost flawless English with her foreign accent sounding attractive with only occasional slightly different pronunciation of some fairly common words.

"Harry and Bill have actually backed me up with my suggestion as they are keenly interested in what is basically my personal story."

"Go on, Marie I'm most intrigued." Gloria could hardly contain her curiousity.

"To help raise more finance to keep the centre flourishing instead of feeling panicky every time there's any big expenditure for its upkeep looming, especially the unforeseen sort, my friends here and I thought we'd turn our interesting conversations during the "cuppa and natter" coffee mornings into a collection of short stories involving our own and other people's experiences in life, that is, people we've known in the past. Alternatively, my life story up to recent times being written as an autobiographical novel which could be published by ourselves as there's a good local printing firm who'd produce a professional piece of work. Money raised from sales of these books could be donated to the centre. In fact there's no reason why both my novel and our short story collection could not be published in the same way."

"Marie's idea, if accepted by the committee, would

put our centre on the map as an example of community spirit in action and we'd also get a unique chance to show our gratitude for all you wonderful staff and volunteers have done for us in so many ways," continued Doreen.

"I think the best idea would be to go ahead with Marie's life story as an autobiography as you say," replied Gloria. "Naturally I'm keen on this idea although the short story series is also a good one. Only, particularly in this instance I feel it's right to warn you, ladies, that you'd have to change the names of characters, locations and mix and match personalities in order to protect individual privacy. The short stories you describe involve basing characters on people you know locally or known in the past who may be still around, even if living in places that are longer distances from here. With a large part of Marie's story taking place abroad I think you'd be on safer ground as, also, many of the characters are now likely to be deceased. Certainly you wouldn't need to be as careful here except perhaps as regards her later life in this country. This is an ambitious project so it's best to concentrate on Marie's story first. Our centre will help you publish it with the local printers you mention or there's some companies on the internet offering online publishing in book form or in the latest electronic book form as a whizz kid device called a kindle. Our manager or any computer literate staff member could check them out to ensure they're genuine."

"I'm sure all of us including staff could share the publishing costs between us," Bill suggested. "Or your financial wizards Messrs Silverwaters and Williamson could find a source of funding towards the cost of producing this book."

"If it sells well, who knows, we might be as successful as the characters in the Calendar Girls film!" Rosemary enthused.

"Hey, steady on, you'll be talking about next step Hollywood!" Harry, the over 60's group's newest member chipped in.

"Anyway while we're on this subject," continued Bill. "We'll have to work out a rota about us all meeting at each other's houses, apart from the once per week cuppa at our centre and work around family commitments as best we can so that we won't miss out on hearing Marie's story. Assuming that it's subject matter will appeal to a wide enough section of the general public we can take it in turns to type it. Doing it on the computer is the best way as it can be easily saved in permanent form in a device called a flash drive."

"I'm so glad I studied and passed that computer skills course then," Rosemary added. "It all started with our local college offering "Computers for the Petrified" sessions, obviously aimed at beginners I went along, gave it a try, found it both interesting and fun so I took to it like a duck to water in a way I'd never thought possible."

"Our Rosie's a real pro, said Harry, admiration evident in his voice.

"Seems she can turn her hand to almost anything.

I'd better get cracking now – never used one on my own yet."

After they all, except Harry, parted company to get on with what were doing for the rest of the day, he lingered on to approach Rosemary, to ask her out for a date, dining at a new stylish local restaurant. Feeling like a teenage boy, hoping to date, for the first time, a girl he liked and wondering whether she'd be attracted to him enough to say yes, his voice sounded faltering and shy. However Rosemary's reaction was similar. She blushed like a schoolgirl being asked out for a first date by a boy she'd greatly fancied and admired but was too self conscious to speak to him directly.

"Yes," she answered. "I'd like that very much, thank you for asking me!"

"Right then tomorrow night it is. Look forward to that!"

When he'd gone Rosemary reflected on Harry's proposal, coming out of the blue, when she'd virtually given up on romance for good and all, being of an age where she felt it was highly unlikely to happen. Having been through a troublesome divorce, many years previous, with another woman involved and a dispute over the custody of their two children had made her wary of forming any romantic attachments to a member of the opposite sex. As it was she was strongly attracted to Harry, all the more because he was obviously romantic, when, like so many in his age group, he could have been mistakenly thinking that romance was finished for couples who'd past the age of 50 and that they would only make themselves the subject of ridicule as regards other people. Rosemary was sorry that this hadn't happened sooner for her, at least when she was 15 or 10 years younger. Still, she reflected, you have to consider yourself jolly fortunate to meet Mr Right at any time in life and it's doubly flattering when you attract a handsome, intelligent man who'd be excellent company and delighted to become romantically involved with you when you're past 55.

Fortunately their date was so enjoyable that, at the

end of the night out, Rosemary felt like she was walking on air and skipped off home like a young girl who'd managed to date the best looking boy in her student tutorial group at college. Her pals and staff at the centre soon noticed that she sparkled in conversation, glowing with happiness. Harry was exactly the same so everyone, including Gloria, was extremely pleased for them. They all felt sure that they'd be attending Rosemary's and Harry's wedding by the following year. Their group began to organize themselves, along with Doreen, Bill and Freda, for meeting regularly with Marie-Claire who had indeed a most interesting, compelling story to tell about her life and personal experiences.

MARIE CLAIRE – MY LIFE STORY
Chapter 1 – Early Days

I was born Marie Claire Jerez. Hereth in Uckel, near Brussels on 9th May 1919. My Spanish surname was pronounced "Hereth."

My mother was a dressmaker and was determined to earn her own living to supplement the modest legacy left by her father, a self-made local small businessman in Antwerp our home town. She succeeded in doing so, as she was a liberated young woman long before the Women's Liberation Movement existed.

My mother, Anna, was a small copper-haired, attractive lady who possessed boundless energy, vitality and a zest for life plainly evident in her bubbly personality. She also had a happy-go-lucky streak which surfaced occasionally. Predictably, she was in the cinema (keen to see the latest silent movie) when I started to be born. There wasn't even time to call an ambulance to take her to the hospital. Instead she was rushed to a nearby friend's home to give birth. My father used to joke with me that I was in such a hurry to enter the world I couldn't even wait until the second house performance!

My father was a skilled carpenter. He could turn any piece of wood into an attractive, functional object that looked like a work of art. His surname was an odd one for a Belgian chap especially one from Antwerp, the main city of the Flanders region and only half an hour by road from the Dutch frontier. Indeed his parents' ancestors were not Flemish at all but Spanish. They had come over to Flanders as refugees from religious persecution namely the Spanish Inquisition during the 16th and early 17th centuries when the Inquisition were persecuting non Catholics whether Protestants, or people from minority faiths or Jews. Some of the refugees stayed in Flanders and some went to England, bringing their various skills with them. These skills included lace-making, weaving and market gardening. It must have been difficult for the Jerez family and their fellow immigrants when Charles, King of Spain, Emperor of the Holy Roman Empire, gave what were then known as the Low Countries (now Holland and Belgium) to his son who became Philip the Second of Spain. Philip brought in The Inquisition as he was a fanatical Catholic and oppressor of the Low Countries. Religious freedom was severely suppressed. The people of Flanders and Holland rebelled in 1566.

Philip sent the Duke of Alba from Spain with a large army who further oppressed the people so much that many Protestants and even the local nobility left the Low Countries. As the Jerezes were still Catholics by the 20th century, from what my father told me, and what had been passed on through the generations of his family, more than likely not all rebels were non-Catholics. The Jerez family must have been loyal to their faith whilst still opposing the cruelty, injustice and intolerance of Spanish rule. Adherence to Catholicism meant that, when the north of the Low Countries declared its independence in 1581, by the Treaty of Utrecht, becoming the Netherlands, the provinces who joined the Netherlands new state re-instated religious tolerance and gradually became Protestant. However the provinces in the south, who did not join the Netherlands, remained Catholic.

The Jerez clan must have been very courageous people. They did well to survive The Inquisition because many rebels were executed or imprisoned and tortured for several years. Sobering reflections which don't bear thinking about for long. They certainly put any minor frustrations or problems which we all experience sometimes in our daily lives into proper perspective .

Marie's small, keenly attentive audience agreed wholeheartedly with those sentiments. She stopped temporarily for a glass of water and then continued: In fact, my former country, Belgium, has a very colourful chequered history, often being a political pawn in European power games stratergised by much larger, more powerful neighbouring states. It was taken over in turn by France, then Austria and finally Holland before becoming an independent Catholic state in 1830. Freedom of religion, association and the press were then guaranteed under our new liberal constitution. The European powers of that time also agreed to guarantee Belgium "perpetual neutrality," ironic in the light of what happened in the two world wars of the 20th century.

"Marie, you should be delivering the next Reith lecture on BBC TV," Bill commented admiringly. "You'll be a celebrity before long!"

"Better late than never," laughed Marie. "Hope it won't take anyone else who's ambitious until they're nearly 82 to achieve whatever they've set their heart on."

"Anyway, your talents are certainly being recognized now," Freda concluded. Marie added, "Understandably, the Jerezes passed down , through their generations and in their psyche, the need to feel and act strongly against attempts to restrict national and religious freedom. They also hated large nations who oppressed smaller ones. They even practised their own individual variation of the Roman Catholic faith rather than following the church's official line. Enough of politics! Normal narrative service resumed!"

As well as his skills as a craftsman, my father was awarded several medals for distinguished service in World War 1. Belgium was in the front line in this war from the first to the final day of conflict. Its geographical position found Belgium most vulnerable to attack from Germany which, of course, was exactly what happened. Germany had to invade Belgium in order to reach and attack France. My father joined a cycling unit as this was another of his talents. (It's all the more odd that I never took to cycling especially with Flanders being so flat, much like neighbouring Holland.) The cyclists had a few advantages over the regular troops in the field. They could get away from the enemy faster and the bikes provided them some protection as they could move more swiftly than foot soldiers and they could speedily throw hand grenades closer to dugouts near enemy lines as they cycled along the way. The hand grenades were actually dropped by parachute from hot air balloons to their contacts on the ground so that they'd be dropped wherever the enemy was located. This was usually achieved by advance information from spies. These hot air balloons also directed and supported the artillery. The cyclist regiment and fledgling air force worked in liaison with each other.

On one occasion the cyclist units joined in with the cavalry, who were known as the 4th and 5th Lansiers and some engineers, all under the command of General De Witte, and ambushed squadrons of the German cavalry at the village of Haelen on 12th August 1914. This feat of derring-do was all the more remarkable as our cavalry men wore breastplates and silver helmets, battledress of a bygone era! As a result, the Germans suffered a serious defeat in Haelen and its surrounding area. For many years onward the silver helmeted force were regarded as legendary heroes. It is interesting to note that Belgium was not the only country in this war to make use of cyclists as support for the infantry. New Zealand, Australia and Britain successfully employed cyclist regiments in a similar way.

Aircraft played an important role in air reconnaissance over the German and Dutch borders to detect movements of German invasion forces. We had our own versions of the famous German Red Baron fighter flying ace. These courageous pioneer pilots were an inspiration to national morale and distinguished themselves in a spectacular way when the Air War gathered momentum during 1916 and 1917. Among our intrepid aces were Willy Coppens who won 37 victories in a single machine gun biplane and, despite being seriously wounded when shooting down his 37th enemy aircraft, managed to land successfully back at his base. Another, Edmund Thiery, achieved 10 victories during 1917-1918 and Fernand Jacquet formed the 'Group de Chasse Jacquet' fighter pilot squadron in February 1918. He gathered together the most skillful flying aces including Coppens and Thiery who, combined with the air forces of Britain and France, finally defeated the enemy in the skies. Additionally, they provided backup force for the army during World War 1.

When I was little, during the 1920's, my father related some exciting stories to me, when sat on his knee, about the adventures of the wartime cyclists units and airmen. He was a good storyteller, sometimes serializing these tales over two nights so that I was kept in suspense until the end of the following day after hearing part one. Usually he always left off at a gripping episode in the tale.

My mother put on an air of rueful, comic exasperation. "Here's me trying to bring Marie up as a lady while you're doing your best to turn her into a rough tomboy. Is she by any chance the son you never had?"

All this took place before Father's disillusionment with patriotism and the Establishment. The latter made him embittered, especially with regard to risking one's life as a young man and then only to experience ingratitude from the government. Sadly, the public had quickly forgotten the courage and sacrifice involved. Indeed it was all deemed relatively unimportant.

You may well wonder how he met my mother in the first place. They met in England in Ilfracombe, North Devon of all places. Mum had fled to England as a refugee from the German invasion. Belgium was historically guaranteed neutrality but this guarantee became useless and Germany used my country as a convenient corridor through which to pass in order to attack our nearest neighbour, France. A London agency was set up to help the refugees with accommodation. It found them somewhere to live, usually with a family who volunteered to take them in. They could find employment locally, being a useful asset, along with Britain's women to fill vacancies with so many men of working age away on active military service. Alternatively, they became helpers within the family circle, a more likely outcome if there were children or old folk in the home. Mum was lucky. The agency placed her in a lovely part of the West country, the picturesque seaside resort of Ilfracombe in Devon. My father came over with an English soldier he'd made friends with when they by chance encountered a British platoon of troops during action on the Western Front. He'd some leave owing to him and, by pure co-incidence, was staying with this new friend who also came from Ilfracombe.

My mother loved it in England. She got on well with the family with whom she'd come to live. One of the practical benefits her father had provided for her was a good education at a fee paying school for girls from middle-class families. The school offered tuition in English and German so she learned to speak and write both languages but found English more fun to learn than German. Therefore, she could easily communicate with her host family. One thing mother noticed about the family she lodged with throughout the war – they lived at a higher standard than most ordinary folk in the area did in those days. This was because, despite the lady's husband being a humble dustman, like mother, his wife ran a thriving business as a quality dressmaker so naturally this increased the family's income.

Her dustman husband was actually very well read despite being forced to leave school when barely 13 years old because his family couldn't afford for him to keep on attending school. He owed his considerable mastery of the English language to regular attendance at the local Methodist Church's Sunday School where there were extra opportunities to add to his basic reading and writing skills learned at school. His wife was very proud of him as his achievements included becoming a Sunday School teacher and a member of the church committee. When my mother's landlady's husband was all dressed up in his best suit for church and special occasions he resembled someone higher up the social scale from himself; in fact more like a bank manager or a senior clerk in local government. They entertained visitors in their "holy of holies" which they christened their back parlour where they kept a small organ. All furniture in there was kept well polished as was the brass hearth surround, coal scuttle, poker and ornaments, all of which sparkled within. My mother thought this was a good advert for Britain in general as, back in Belgium in those days you could easily distinguish a working class person from their superiors within the class system. Few ordinary folk back home had the opportunity to rise above their humble position in society.

"Rather a unique view of British society in the early years of the 20th century!" Freda commented.

"Yes, it's sometimes astonishing how any outsider looking into a community, family circle or whatever can interpret the social setups so differently from those closely involved."

After that reply, Marie and friends closed their meeting and agreed to reconvene during the following week. Marie opened their next session by announcing that her story will become more interesting and exciting from then onwards.

To continue about my mother's experiences as a refugee in England during World War 1:

Anna, my adventurous mother, also nearly joined the Suffragette Movement when they staged a rally in the centre of London when she arrived in England. She'd never seen anything like this back home and had only heard stories handed down via her grandfather now long deceased, about the Belgium Revolution of 1830 in which the country declared its independence from the Netherlands. In these tales, rowdy street scenes, protests which had the potential for becoming violent and fiery speeches prevailed but, fortunately, apart from a few isolated brawls there was very little bloodshed. It was all over in a relatively short time.

Therefore, she was somewhat alarmed and bewildered at first. Anna listened to a couple of speeches by the Pankhurst sisters and, when another bystander who sympathized with the cause, translated a few of the longer words used which she'd not quite understood, she found she agreed with the protesters' aims and whole-heartedly wished them luck. My mother never did anything half-heartedly. She had a wonderful zest for life. The only aspect of it she was less than enthusiastic about was housework – she found it boring and a bind. Don't all of us women do sometimes!

However, despite her genuine interest and sympathy for the suffragette cause, England was, after all, not her country and she was still planning to return home to Belgium after the war had ended. Following a whirlwind romance with my father they married in 1918 in Ilfracombe. My mother wore a dark green silk two-piece with a spray of bright peach coloured roses on one jacket lapel and my father wore a smart, grey suit. On their wedding photo they looked a most happy, carefree young couple.

When they returned to Belgium there was "a bit of a barney" locally after I was born because it appeared that father used to have a steady girlfriend before the war. It was understood by the girl's family that they would marry eventually. However my father was only 24 when he married mother (he was four years younger than she) so, as he said, he'd been really too young and inexperienced to know his own mind when courting Hortense. The war had unsettled him, so he maintained, and other, more interesting opportunities were presenting themselves for him. My mother represented someone more exciting and life-enhancing than the girl next door. He'd obviously been bowled over by her lively personality, attractive appearance and independent spirit, the latter phenomenon not often encountered amongst middle-class ladies in those days. The girl he'd ditched for my mum made a scene in our street when she saw Mum with me in my pram. However, it was too late for the girl to reverse the situation in her favour. We never saw or heard anything further from her after that incident so we could only hope that she had better luck with romance the next time round.

To return to the present: As was previously mentioned, the five friends (the original four being increased to five by the inclusion of Harry) arranged to spend regular sessions with Marie, either at the social club or at each other's homes. On this occasion they met at Doreen and Bill's neat, homely terraced house, close to the town centre. Harry drew attention to himself by politely clearing his throat, preparing to bring up some relevant news about their project.

"I'm sure we're all intrigued by what we've heard about your family history so far Marie but there's something I need to mention right now. The fact is I've been offered a part-time job. An old school chum of mine is retiring soon so he mentioned me to Mr Dobson who runs our local hardware shop. Mr Dobson is very much in favour of employing older people. He reckons they're more reliable and delighted to be taken on, so my interview led to my being offered an assistant's job, serving in the shop for 4 mornings per week and to cover for every other Saturday in each month, holidays or sickness relief, etc. This'll be why I won't be joining you in the mornings except for

Wednesdays when the shop is closed all day. If ever we meet on a Saturday I could come along if I have one free. There's not many job opportunities for folk of retirement age in Torr Brookdale, it being only a small town, so I'm lucky to have this chance of earning some regular supplementary income. I felt I should go for it. This way I can also be more generous towards friends and family, especially my super new friend, Rosemary, have extra money for holidays outings and unforeseen expenditures which often seems to occur when one's finances are not at their best."

"I'm sure we all understand," Marie replied and added, "You'll be very welcome anyway to join us whenever you can."

"Any sessions you miss, Harry, I'll send you the relevant copies of the installments which I'll have typed out via my computer. All that typing and editing of Marie's book will keep me out of mischief," said Rosemary with a chuckle in her voice. "It must have been a job and a half for you to have written your life story by hand. Thanks for having it photocopied or, with me never having learned shorthand, we'd have been on this project for half a decade!"

"This is also a convenient point at which to finish for today," Freda concluded. "I've got so carried away with our project that I almost forgot – must hurry to school to pick up Phoebe." Phoebe was Freda's granddaughter, now attending the local primary school. Freda occasionally met Phoebe after school and took her home when her daughter wasn't available to do so.

"Remember that my house is where our next meeting will be. You'll be pleased to know that since I've bought my new breadmaker, it's so versatile that I can make a great variety of loaves, buns and teacakes. Can't beat homemade ones. Bet you'd like to sample some Belgian buns with your cuppa."

The others gave her wry smiles and chuckles as if to say "Very appropriate!"

Marie's narrative was resumed when they met at Freda's home, a couple of days later.

To recap: My parents returned to Belgium shortly after World 1 had ended and settled back in their home city of Antwerp. Everyone round the neighbourhood soon knew Anna was back with a vengeance as she was the first woman in Antwerp to go about in public wearing a short skirt. It was around fourteen months after I was born that she'd been studying the fashion scene and concluded that the staid, conservative province of Flandria needed to be catapulted into the 20th century where women, she believed, had a more active, less restricted role to play in society than in former times. I still have a photo of her wearing that short skirt and frothy lace flappers' top in bright peach pink. Her outfit attracted a crowd. Mum's escapade was also in our local Antwerp newspaper. It sparked off the disapproval and moral censure of the older women who'd already labeled her as brazen, definitely on the slippery slope towards easy virtue. At best they thought her a vulgar exhibitionist.

However, within the next few weeks, first the

young women, then the middle-aged and finally the elderly ones went around in knee-length or shorter skirts. Long skirts and dresses were then consigned to the pages of history, formal balls and grand occasions attended by royalty, aristocracy, the wealthy and famous.

Chapter 2 – Early Experiences

Despite the war having ravaged farmlands, the southern coalfields in Wallonia and nearly destroyed the important junction town of Ypres in the West Flanders, the country recovered relatively well, and our end, the north became more prosperous than the south. This was because of more scientific farming methods boosting agricultural productivity and new light industries were developing round the port area of Antwerp. For most of the 1920's prosperity reigned at least in the north-east of Belgium until the Wall Street crash in the USA in 1929. Then, like most of the western world, economic depression, the bleak years of unemployment and poverty rendered disillusionment with government being rife.

Whatever transpired in life and in the outside world, my parents, Anna and Eugene, dealt with it; not always wisely but mostly as best they could. They were colourful characters. In the earlier years of their marriage they held parties at our house when the place filled with guests consisting of mother's numerous friends and a few of my father's old comrades who'd survived the Western Front. When, at one such party, my parents thought I was safely tucked up in bed for the night as, at the time I was only just four years old, I crept downstairs without anyone noticing and drank a whole bottle of Spanish burgundy wine. My mother, although bright and full of vitality, was sometimes scatter-brained and, on this occasion, she must have forgotten to lock the drinks cabinet. When they and one of the guests noticed that I was dancing round like a small spinning top, singing my head off and swinging dangerously on the banister, I was restrained. It took some time to recover the offending bottle as I'd hidden it, thinking how clever I was. Eventually, I threw up, bringing up the remains of my last meal and hot milk drink, was settled down and, apart from a nasty headache, a visit and treatment from the doctor, I fully recovered from my venture into the adult world.

I was seven years old before I attended school but this was no disadvantage as mother taught me to tell the time, basic reading and writing: also simple arithmetic which you would be likely to use in everyday life. At that time you usually stayed in the same school from ages 7-16, moving up to the Seniors Department at age eleven. When I was eleven I was sent to a private school called Belle Pare' which had, according to mother's relations, an excellent reputation. However I spent a most unhappy two years there and had to leave in disgrace. I soon found out that it was French-biased in language and culture. Several times I was in trouble with the staff for speaking Flemish. "Honestly friends, some of the pupils were the limit." Marie paused as Freda, Rosemary, Doreen, Bill and Gloria (Harry was absent from this meeting because of starting his new job) listened intently as her face flushed, even after a lifetime, at the unpleasant recollection. "There are few things in life worse than catty, spiteful girls. Well, this nasty contingent often made unkind fun of me as I also went through a stage of being clumsy as well as continuing to speak Flemish whenever possible. Finally, when I was humiliated in front of the class by the deputy head that was the last straw. Fortunately, my parents, who by now were not surprised by what was happening at that school, took me away from there without further hesitation.

"I expect there was an inquest about the matter back home then," Gloria commented.

"Yes, Gloria, it did cause quite a stir. My father, who was more against the Belgian state than mother was, took an "I told you so" stance with her. He declared he was never in favour of my attending Belle Pare' and had a row on the subject next with her relatives who, he thought, fancied themselves as though they were aristocracy instead of upstart, bourgeois trades people. Anyway, one of my father's folk, Aunt Fanny, whom I liked very much because she was a just and kindly person, settled the matter by praising me for having the moral courage to make a stand for freedom of speech and supporting our nation's underdogs, who were often discriminated against in education and employment which, in one so young was highly commendable. Father's relations, like mother's were fully supportive of the Flemish cause although, within our family circle, those on my father's side tended to be more vocal about it. Aunt Fanny also pointed out that anyone could be mistaken once in a while about any issue life could confront you with. After all my parents only wanted what was best for me so it was unfair to blame each other for an unfortunate outcome.

After that, as far as school was concerned, I truly turned a corner as I then attended a local Roman Catholic school run by nuns with Mother Superior as the head. In time I made several good friends there, being so much happier than at my former school. The nuns were excellent teachers. We even learned English there as a third language on the curriculum so I learned to speak and write English fairly well.

During the earlier years of my childhood, my parents were a happy, united couple until I was about nine and a half-years' old. What happened then caused distrust on mother's side which never completely cleared from their relationship.

My father's expert knowledge and skill with woodwork, carpentry and furniture landed him a good job as a sales representative for a Dutch firm which dealt in fine furniture. His work took him to some cities in our country including the southern half known as Wallonia. He was a loyal employee for at least seven years. It was his roving eye for the ladies that lead to his downfall. Sometimes there were a couple of days' delay in his return home but mother had no reason for suspicion until a friend of our family, who worked for the same company, discovered, by chance, a piece of elegant jewellery in a presentation box, fall out of a drawer in the desk where father kept his paperwork. On that occasion, father managed to explain why the jewellery was there. His explanation was a pleasant surprise for mother that he temporarily forgot to give her due to being extra busy at work. Soon after this incident, a mix-up over the time at which father should have returned from one of his business trips made both his colleague and my mother become suspicious.

Mother confronted father with this and he finally admitted he'd been having an affair with a woman who lived in a suburb south of Brussels. Mother was so hurt that she told the boss of his firm, a Dutchman, Pieter van der Ryden, who was well known for his strong sense of morality both in public and private life. Looking back, although had this happened to me, I would have been just as upset and disgusted at his deceit and betrayal of trust, I doubt if I would have gone off so impulsively to my husband's boss about it especially as it would not have helped either of us to have him sacked, which, in this case, was exactly what happened. This led to father's long-term unemployment so he paid a heavy price for his adultery.

Fortunately my father's folks were the first to learn

of my parents' temporary break-up. My mother's family had never fully approved of her choice of marriage partner so they would have judged him more severely and there would have been an almighty row taking place. Blind Auntie Louise, who was the psychic sage of my cousin Roger's family, the Van Meikles and whose sixth sense she claimed, was God's compensation for her premature blindness, reckoned it would have been better if she'd stayed on her own with me and not taken him back as she did after a year's separation. However, mother's strong sense of morality meant that she would not break her marriage vows. She also thought that it was a more stable environment for me to have both parents living with me instead of just one and the other visiting us occasionally. At that time I very much wanted my Dad back so we would be a proper family again, but I regretted this decision when I grew up.

Chapter 3 – Growing Up

The Great Depression in the 1930's resulted in my father never finding full-time employment until the Second World War. He just did one-off sporadic carpentry jobs in peoples homes whenever these opportunities arose. They were often few and far between, because household budgets were tighter than in the previous decade. Sometimes he helped mother with running her business. However, he hated her being the main breadwinner in our little household. The tough male provider situation was not purely an aspect of British culture. It was accepted as the norm in Western Europe, as well, in those days. He did not, however, fortunately blame her because she had, at least, forgiven him for his infidelity and kept to her marriage vows. He blamed the Belgian State and its representatives, the government of the day. This led him into being in sympathy with a dangerous, sinister form of politics.

More about that later in my story.

Through the stormy waters of my parents' marriage and their financially insecure life, I was determined to plan my adult life so that if and when I married and had children, they would not have to endure emotional and financial insecurity with the battle to clear off mounting debts that marred a big chunk of my later childhood and youth. Fortunately, though, there were some joyous, sunny experiences, humorous ones too, fun at home and during my courting episodes as they called it in those days and a couple of hair-raising, narrow escapes from death or detention involving certain slave labour during the dark days when our country was under Nazi occupation in World War 11.

Doreen, Gloria and the other friends, eager to hear the next chapter in Marie's story, asked her what she did after leaving school. Marie replied thus: "Oh, I kept house for my Mum to enable her to run her dressmaking business. This suited her fine as she'd never been keen on housework. Also, for all our sakes she needed to concentrate full-time on the business to develop regular trade because of the grim economic slump in those days."

"Yet, you're such an intelligent person with really scintillating conversation," Rosemary marveled. "You speak better English than some of our people who've lived in England all their lives. I bet you could have secured a good, well-paid job if such an opportunity came your way."

"It's nice of you to have such a good opinion of my abilities but the fact was in those days in Belgium, any girl from a middle class background with the appropriate education as well was brought up to be a lady with the result that, when you left school, you knew bits about most subjects but not enough about one to enable you to earn a living.

As my parents struggled to keep up appearances as middle class Antwerp citizens, sometimes without the financial means to do so, further and higher education was out of the question. Same as here, before the Second World War, the family had to pay for it themselves.

This was why parents and other relatives encouraged you to find a regular, steady boyfriend once you'd reached the age of eighteen. Marriage was a good way out of being stuck in some dead-end job which you'd have to give up anyway once you were married. Some very old-fashioned parents stubbornly thought that only girls from poor, working class backgrounds needed to find employment so they supported their daughters financially while match-making whenever eligible young men were around. If only we'd a higher income to fund career-based further education, I'd liked to pursue a career in local government or a lawyer or a politician's secretary as politics, government and the law always interested me then and I always did well at school in those subjects in spite of having to work extra hard with spelling which was my only difficulty when doing written work. In schools in Belgium, we were taught our basic legal rights and how we were governed, both locally and nationally."

"Aye, I believe that's the way they do things in education over on the continent," Bill remarked. "Seems very sensible to me especially as folk now lead more complicated lives where money and relationships are concerned."

"I'd better not divorce you then," Doreen joked. "Though you do have a point there. Unfortunately, legal problems are more likely to crop up during one's lifetime, more so than in the past. I'm inclined to think that the Law Society, which are the solicitors' trade union, won't like the notion of a large number of intelligent, well-educated people deciding to conduct their own cases in court if they've sufficient time to prepare them and confident enough to believe they'll win. It'd have to be confined to straight-forward cases which the average person would be most likely to experience."

"Like your English mortgages," Marie replied

ruefully. "They seem to be more trouble than they're worth. In my ex-country, people usually live in decent standard rented accommodation. Only the wealthy buy their own homes. I believe it's the same in Holland and Germany."

"Yes, in many ways our European neighbours seem to have more common sense on important aspects of daily life than we have," said Freda. "What with all the bills householders have to pay, plus taxes on top, it must be a struggle to pay mortgages as well especially if anything goes wrong such as unemployment, illness, accidents, etc. Insurance against any of these unwelcome happenings is also added expense."

"A delicate balance to maintain I'm sure," Marie agreed.

"My, we have strayed a long way from your story," chuckled Harry who, on this occasion was able to join them because of some unforeseen time off work.

"Now where were we? I think you'd left school and were helping your Mum at home."

"Yes," added Rosemary "You mentioned in detail your Belgian marriage market. It sounds like something straight from a Jane Austen novel with girls and their parents scheming and trying their best to attract eligible gentlemen for future husbands."

"Did you go along with the conventional viewpoint of your society in those times?" asked Doreen.

"Up to a point, yes," was Marie's rueful reply. "It was my dream, like many a local girl in those days to find Mr Right, fall in love, marry and live happily ever after. Except that, of course, dating and developing relationships does not always run smoothly or guarantee a happy ending just when we'd like. This was certainly the case where I was concerned. Looking back, if I had my time again, I wouldn't have made marriage my main goal as a young woman or have fallen into a narrow way of thinking, whereby you feel you must take major steps and achieve certain things in life by the time you've reached age forty at the latest, otherwise it's too late to fulfill your dreams or ambitions so you end up spending the rest of your life stuck in a humdrum rut."

To continue my story: I remember that when I was eighteen, I went to my first special "coming out debut dance" at our city hall. I was wearing a fancy turquoise taffeta dress mother made for me but I found very few partners and had to sit out more dances than anticipated which naturally was disappointing and frustrating. At that time I was rather shy and self-conscious, trying too hard to make a good impression. I felt awkward amidst the bubbly, super-confident girls who seemed to be so good at small talk and quick witted replies when conversation flowed. One particular girl, Brigitte, had young men buzzing round her like bees around garden flowers. She was half-French, vivacious and attractive in a sensual way. She was what mother would describe as forward and brash. I decided later, on mother's advice which, on this occasion, was right, that I would, in future, be myself, try to cultivate interesting conversation, and also be a good listener to show I was really interested in a young man as a special individual with talents to offer. In other words the emphasis on being friendly instead of seeing him purely as a potential husband.

A year later, when I went with family and friends to another local dance, this was a much more successful, happier occasion than the last one. I wore a simple, black satin dress which was nevertheless stylish. It suited me well, being an attractive contrast to my blonde hair. It was a wonderful night out. I did well for dancing partners. One who was particularly attentive was a young man called Hendrik Varens. He was a local lad whom I already knew a bit by sight. His mother was Dutch. She was the senior district nurse in our city. We occasionally saw her pedaling away, in all weathers, on an ancient but trusty bicycle. It would certainly be a quaint, museum piece these days! What a contrast when now you see professional ladies in their cars with their mobile phones, laptops, Ipods and God knows what other technological paraphernalia. Don't know they're born! Might not keep as physically fit though."

Anyway to return to my story: Little did we know then that Hendrik would try to develop a sinister influence on my father which also caused me to make a life-changing decision for myself.

Chapter 4 – First Romance

Gloria became more and more intrigued by Marie's life story. She felt almost the same feeling of excitement as children experience close to Christmas. Her thoughts ran thus: If Marie's book proves to be successful and achieves popularity with a wide section of the general public, this would be a great boost to our club as stories of grand and great-grand parents' experiences bring modern history to life in a way that no textbook or encyclopedia ever can. These days they often seem to be in big demand as they're usually a most interesting read. Anything like this would surely strengthen our case for keeping the club open and thriving. Over and above this, our management team, friends, neighbours and club regulars have found a new friend cum supporter from whom our community can really benefit. We must ensure that we do not use her for a good, saleable book to help save our club and then scarcely keep in touch.

She's proving to be a loyal friend well worth having.

"Do continue," Gloria added enthusiastically. Marie Claire resumed her narrative.

"After all these years it's a relief to get some details of my past off my chest as, apart from Pete and my family in England, I've kept them to myself. No one else here ever knew about them.

Looking back now, I'm so relieved that I followed my own instincts and that mother didn't pressurize me into engagement and marriage to Hendrik. In fact I was briefly engaged to Hendrik when I was nearly twenty. We were to be married within a year following our engagement. You'll see why in due course that I thanked God I never took that final step. In those days, respectable, middle-class people and the better end of the working class regarded betrothal as a serious commitment which no couple embarked upon unless you were both very sure of each other's feelings and compatibility. It took some considerable moral courage to break off a virtual promise to marry if you'd any doubts in your mind regarding your overall relationship. The only exception to these rules was if you discovered something appalling in your man's past that would entitle you to break with him. It would have to be something like confession to a murder, bigamy or hereditary mental illness involving violent tendencies for you to escape your obligation.

To return to when I was nineteen – the period from the night of the dance to roughly another year and a quarter; I was absolutely bowled over by Hendrik as, at that time, he was the most attractive chap I'd ever come across. He was tall with blond hair, a good talker with a forceful personality. He'd travelled abroad quite a lot compared with most people we knew, having been to Germany, Austria, Northern France, Denmark, Poland and Luxembourg as a rep for a new, flourishing company which sold agricultural machinery. To me he seemed exciting, dynamic, the height of sophistication, a scintillating conversationalist, charming and romantic enough to sweep a girl off her feet. He gave me my first taste of sexual attraction between a woman and a man. I was doubly flattered as I was no great beauty – for a start I'd sandy eyebrows, a hooked nose that I'd always regarded as too large in proportion to my face and mousy light brown eye lashes which I had to touch up with mascara to make them look more attractive. My best features were my wavy ash blonde hair and a shapely, but trim, figure. I also tended to be rather quiet when newly introduced to a stranger until I got to know them better and became more used to their company.

When I got to know Hendrik better I found him rather possessive and suspicious-minded, particularly when he was away on company business and we didn't see each other for a week or two. On his return, he questioned me about where I'd been and who I'd been with. Probably because my cousin Roger was a handsome young man with a friendly personality, Hendrik was also jealous of us meeting up occasionally as my family and Roger's were close friends. Roger sometimes invited me to join his group of friends, as we were all young people who enjoyed occasional nights out, to the local cinemas, theatres or dance halls or boat trips along the canal at Bruges. In summertime, we all enjoyed a couple of day trips to the nearest seaside resorts of Ostend or Blankenberg. Everyone in our neighbourhood knew that Roger and I were just chums – he was no more a rival than my female friends: in fact just as harmless. Hendrik, with being local, should also have known this as I'd never been secretive about it.

One of my regular girl friends, Simone, seemed to envy me because she thought Hendrik's adoration and devotion must be making me feel super attractive and very special. I pointed out to her that, while this would appear to be very flattering to the female ego, a girl still needed some outside interests, social activities and some friends of her own sex to meet up for an occasional shopping trip, a coffee and a chat, some laughs together – in all, some freedom and time to herself. In fact, because of his over-possessiveness plus dangerous political views, I decided against marrying him. I then broke off our engagement.

This caused a drama locally with mother being so well known in our district. Our relatives and friends were divided into camps for and against Hendrik, pro and anti me. A couple of my more prim and conventional aunts and a few of my sixteen cousins sniffed: "That Jerez girl should know her own mind by now – after all she's had several boyfriends and she's been going with Hendrik for over a year. Dosen't know what she does want, if you ask me!"

My mother, who usually had an answer for everything retorted: "You should know that Hendrik was the first steady boyfriend she's had – after all she's still very young. Breaking off an engagement is far preferable to marrying the wrong one."

My aunt, Liliane, who had an acid tongue and whom my father couldn't stand, had the nerve to chip in with, "And we all know who married the wrong one because she flirted for far too long. Definitely had too high expectations which no man could hope to aspire to!"

Mum just told her sharply to mind her own business and flounced off the scene.

"It sounds just like Continental Coronation St where you lived," chuckled Harry. "Your other reason for finishing with Hendrik rather intrigues me – the dangerous political views. What were they and why did they have the potential to be a bad influence on your father?"

"This is one part of my life I've been reluctant to talk about in a very long time for fear of misunderstandings arising among my new family and circle of friends, acquaintances, etc especially with coming to live in England barely two years after the war had ended."

Marie then closed the meeting, announcing the next one to be held at Freda's house with the inviting prospect of best quality ground coffee and Belgian buns, supplied by Marie, being served for refreshments.

"Very appropriate," Gloria laughed. "We all

second that!"

Chapter 5 – Politics and Controversy

Marie continued relating her story to her enthusiastic audience.

"Hendrik, as I've described was quite a forceful personality and so was my father, though in a less obvious way. When Hendrik and I were courting, as they referred to this activity in those days, he occasionally visited us at our home. He often chatted at length with my father as they'd a fair amount in common. Both of them were interested in antique furniture, woodwork, football (they both supported our local team, Anderlect) and politics.

They were both Flemish Nationalists so sometimes they had a grumbling session about the injustices imposed, by the Belgian State, on the Flemish majority in the north of our country. Despite sacrifices made in the trenches by Flanders during World War 1 and our bearing the brunt of German attacks on our towns and villages (Ypres was nearly destroyed during that terrible war) we all felt that we still hadn't won fair representation in the post-war government. French-speaking Belgians, namely the Walloons, Hendrik and Dad agreed, always achieved higher social status, better education and jobs, often better quality housing. Although, in spite of the 1930's Depression, the economic situation for us Flandrians was improving, giving us more power to change the political scene in our favour, we were still looked down upon by French-speaking government officials, professional people within commerce, the arts and culture.

You were categorized as country bumpkins and near morons if you spoke Flemish as your first language. Father repeated to Hendrik what we sometimes heard from him when he felt bitter and frustrated about being unemployed for so long.

"In defence of our country, we Flandrians risked our lives daily and many lost their lives including some of my good friends. When I did my infantry stint in the trenches, before I joined the cycle/balloon regiment, you often found a fellow soldier dead next to you at first light of dawn. Once, in self-defence, I had to bayonet a young German soldier in hand to hand combat. I was a fraction quicker in handling the weapon so I killed the enemy soldier. It haunted my mind for a long time afterwards. The lad couldn't have been more than 19 years old, at the most.

When we held our veterans parade a couple of years ago, believe it or not, the youngsters jeered at us. The socialists attacked us in the press and on the radio. They made us out to be at worst, violent thugs, at best, morons who believed everything a shower of war-mongering politicians fed to us. To crown it all, the government of our caring Belgian state, wouldn't even ensure that reliable, permanent employment was available for us."

Mother, who wished to convey to me and any visitors on the scene, a more balanced picture of our recent history, pointed out that Wallonia too was devastated by the enemy, indeed their coal and steel industries had never fully recovered to this day. Accusations from Hendrik and Dad of "whose side are you on?" quickly turned into an argument which I usually managed to diffuse before too many sparks flew around.

On a few other occasions, they discussed what was sometimes referred to in the popular press as "the Jewish problem." A great many Jews had fled from Germany or later on from Austria, to Belgium, Holland, Britain and other "friendly" countries as refugees from Nazi persecution so they received a fair amount of sympathy in our city. There were also Jewish economic refugees from some parts of Eastern Europe. They'd come over from Poland, Russia and Czechoslovakia where they were poverty stricken, hoping to find a better standard of living in the west. Hendrik seemed very prejudiced against them, even those who'd escaped from racial and religious intolerance. He tried to influence my dad against them, saying that even those who had lived in Belgium for two or more generations should be deported to Israel or else sent to some remote part of the world where they wouldn't aggravate the already grim unemployment problem in our country. Other countries in Western Europe were, of course, equally hard hit.

At other times, they discussed the other controversial subject on many people's minds in Belgium in those times, the Spanish Civil War which raged on through the decade. Many young men, faced with long term unemployment went off to fight in Spain on one side or the other. (Their other option was the police force). Of course, Hendrik was quick to point out that the ordinary working people's brigade was riddled with Communists so, if one did not wish to end up being dominated by the Soviet regime which most people in our nation would not want, Franco's cause was the one to back. I didn't feel sufficiently qualified to speak on this grave matter as, at that time I did not have much interest in politics other than supporting the

Flemish Nationalists. My focus was to hope that this new dreadful war would be soon brought to an end as nothing good seemed to emerge from it.

Fortunately Hendrik never succeeded in brain-washing father completely, but just made him more resentful of the economic refugees who crowded our city parks with their prolific families. They always appeared to make a reasonably good living, either honestly or dishonestly. With father, they were just an additional source of frustration. However, he would not have harmed the Jews although they were not his favourite people. Sporadic snippets of conversation between Hendrik and father, overheard by mother, made her strongly suspect that Hendrik's outlook on life was decidedly Fascist. When convinced of this, she tried, in a subtle way, to discourage their friendship. She was greatly relieved when I broke off our engagement as she had begun to dread having him as a son-in-law.

Marie finished with announcing: "In the next meeting I'll tell you about mother's Jewish friends and some entertaining experiences with them back then."

Chapter 6 – A Family Friend

Mother heartily disliked Hendrik. The main reason for her disliking him was his condemnation of the Jews. She had a Jewish friend, originally from Poland, Martha Szarv who, like Mum, worked in the clothing trade. Madame Szarv had two daughters, Leah and Elizabeth. Leah, who, round about my age, was one of my circle of friends, while Elizabeth was three years younger. Like their mother, they were lively, fun-loving personalities and really good company.

Madame Szarv ran a small dress design and haute' couturier` business (stylish, high-class French dressmaking) on the other side of Antwerp near the small town of St Nicklaus. She often came into our city for coffee and cakes at one of the many attractive café bars. She enjoyed a chat with Mum on these occasions, as it was an ideal opportunity for Martha to catch up with local news. They also discussed the latest gossip in our area. Most people in Antwerp liked and admired Martha because, as a widow with two children, she managed so well in bringing them up to be decent, honest and very likeable girls and she ran her own successful business. She worked hard to set this business up herself. Things became easier for her when she could finally afford to employ a couple of assistants, a trainee and a clerk-cum-receptionist who organized the appointments and paperwork. Martha was such a cheerful, positive person that some women envied her independent spirit and financial freedom. They thought her ultra- modern lifestyle was well worth aspiring to.

However, sometimes the grass isn't always as green on the other side as many of us may imagine and, although still only about forty, Martha had been totally committed to building her business and caring for her daughters so she'd had virtually no time and very few opportunities for romance. Her independent spirit made her determined not to marry just for financial security and a father for her girls. This was mainly because her marriage had been a real love match. Mother suspected that she'd never succeed in finding anyone as good or could make her as happy as her late husband had done.

Martha and Mother were certainly the dynamic duo! They were both lively, spirited and attractive. They embraced creativity. Both showed the same liberal, outgoing attitude to life. It was no wonder they got on so well together. Of the two, Mum was somewhat more conventional in outlook and more straight-laced. She put a higher value on respectability but otherwise they complemented each other ideally. Martha's qualities of courage and determination in the face of adversity would be much needed in the not-too-distant future when she and her little family would face deadly danger during the Nazi occupation. Should they be subjected to abuse and intimidation we knew she would never give the Nazis the satisfaction of seeing her broken in spirit. However, that's another story you'll hear about in due course.

After this installment, the usual contingent of

committee members, regular users and visiting committee groups from the social club in the nearby town of Falcondale, plus those from the village hall at Badgers' Rise all met at Torr Brookdale centre for a special meeting to discuss their latest fund-raising ideas. Marie-Claire's story plan was mooted, along with many other ideas, some imaginative but nevertheless workable. Some ideas were whacky, fun-packed and some, just plain bizarre. They all agreed to keep on with the preparation and eventual publication of Marie-Claire's book, having found a story of real human interest that their club's supporters with their lively, inquiring minds who obviously enjoyed varied reading matter could recommend the book to many local people. It would also have appeal much further afield in more far-flung parts of the county. Therefore, they concluded, it was going to be most saleable. Gloria, Joe and the friends were naturally delighted with this outcome.

Chapter 7 – A Comic Episode

The five friends, together with Gloria, met up with Marie at her home for the first time. The females in the friends' circle were impressed with the bright, bold colours Marie had chosen for her soft furnishings. Wicker and bamboo light furniture gave her rooms an all year-round summery look. Gloria concluded: "You're a most imaginative homemaker , Marie!"

"You've just gained yourself a new career," Freda chipped in. "You can come and re-design my place. Bet you'd win a prize in one of those glossy home and garden magazine comps!"

After exchanging banter, small talk and jokes, Marie continued her story where she'd left off, about herself and her Mother's Jewish friends from before World War 2.

"Amongst Mother's numerous friends and relatives, one of her cousins worked as a ship's pilot on the Schelde, that great waterway between East Flanders and Holland. Rotterdam, to be exact. He used to tell her some interesting tales about the seamen, including those who'd served on the merchant ships, especially their experiences in exotic, faraway places, which in those days were just names to ordinary folk or, at best, settings for adventure yarns or romantic stories enjoyed from novels. It transpired that this knowledge gained from the pilot and one of the captains came in very useful, on one occasion it saved her from considerable embarrassment.

Anna, my Mother, invited Martha and her girls to supper one evening as we'd both been at Martha's home several times and mother wished to return her friend's hospitality. She wanted to prepare a more unusual, exciting meal for her guests. As we'd had fish (living in a port city with the coast so near, fish was always cheap and plentiful), lamb, beef and omelettes within that same month, mother started preparing a foreign dish – a British one which consisted of hot bacon sandwiches combined with other tasty ingredients in them. These were mushrooms, scrambled eggs and sliced onions. The sandwiches were finally topped with grated cheese browned under our charcoal grill of which mother was very proud. She put them in the oven, keeping warm, ready for our guests who were due to arrive shortly. She even added a professional touch to the meal – having ready a Delft blue pottery dish, displaying fresh, mixed herbs for the garnish.

At that point, I'd been away, visiting our relatives in Ghent, having just returned home when mother was popping the sandwiches in the oven. "Now with any guests other than Martha & Co, this would have been fine, Mum. But here you've really put the cat among the pigeons. Bacon ones! Of all the savoury specials you could have made, you had to choose those with bacon. In case you've forgotten, Martha and family are Jewish. Hope to goodness Izzy won't find out!"

Izak Goldovsky, who was originally from Poland and a refugee from religious intolerance, had made his new home in Antwerp. He was a popular figure both among the Jewish and Gentile communities. Affectionately known as Zacky, he was a kind, friendly, father-like personality but his easy going manner belied his formidable reputation for insisting on strict adherence to the rules of Judaism. Mother nearly panicked but she was adept at concealing her unease at her mistake. In father's opinion she was a frustrated actress, missing her chance of a stage career only because her elders, within her respectable bourgeois background, had disapproved of any precarious occupation especially one coupled with temptations to succumb to an immoral lifestyle.

She chatted, laughed and joked with our friends whilst calmly serving the sandwiches. They praised her up to no end about the delicious food, proclaiming enthusiastically how tasty it was and questioned mother about it when they'd finished their meal.

"Where can we buy some? How much does it cost? How do you cook it?"

"Well I'd better satisfy your curiousity." Mum then proceeded with a clever tall story. I just had to admire her quick-wittedness in the circumstances.

"It's a very rare meat from a wild mammal of the South Sea Islands, Fiji, Tonga, Western Samoa, that area. The animal is a cross between a wallaby and a lemur. The natives often preserve their flesh in salt so that's what you've tasted tonight. Devilish difficult to get hold of the stuff as the creatures move so fast. Hunters have their work cut out to capture them. These animals tend to be nocturnal so the natives have a struggle at night time, trying to catch them. Therefore, the meat is an expensive delicacy, a once-in-a-while treat. Sorry, but that's the situation."

Father and I had a laugh together after they'd gone. "Your mother always has an answer to everything. When she couples it with some romancing, she'd make a good actress or a politician. Sounds very eloquent and convincing. What do you reckon, Marie, that she's wasted as a suburban dressmaker?"

Mother, like myself, hoped that Rabbi Zacky would not discover that three members of his flock had unwittingly been eating unclean, un-Kosher food as guests of a well-known Antwerp personality. Mother actually did run into Rabbi Zacky in town. He greeted her in his usual good-humoured way. "I hear you enjoy entertaining new friends in your home occasionally, especially those who like to try a more exciting variety of cuisine."

Mum swore that he winked at her. His expression said it all. "By Jove, you're a case Madame Jerez – you're a mischievous schoolgirl, a scatterbrain and a laugh a minute, all rolled into one. What would our city do without its resident comedienne!"

Despite being orthodox in his faith, a strict authoritarian in his post, Zacky possessed a first-rate sense of humour. Like Martha, he would need that and great courage, also endurance for the dangers, suffering troubles and challenges which certainly would materialize for them in the not-too-distant future.

Chapter 8 – More Eventful Days

Somehow we always managed to get involved or end up as spectators when my mother took on the role of neighbourhood agony aunt, trying to solve the problems of relatives and friends within our community. Mum was one of those people whose own business was the last she should mind. However, this was part of her generous, warm-hearted nature: a genuine desire to help others even though sometimes inconvenient for her to do so. She unofficially counseled two of cousin Roger's elder brothers when their marriages broke up: Carel's as a result of the war and occupation of our country which, in their case, rendered their relationship unstable and Max's as the outcome of incompatibility.

Max's marital troubles were more publicly high profile than those of Carel's because the latter was a more private person with an ordinary hospital admin job. Max achieved local fame as a successful actor and programme presenter on Radio Antwerp. He married a local school teacher, Denise, who came from a lower middle-class respectable background where the virtues of self-discipline and thrift were regarded as vitally important. Through his radio work, Max met and fell in love with a glamorous actress who was developing a successful stage career in both Belgium and neighbouring Luxembourg. There was an almighty row when his wife, Denise, found out about their relationship but to give Rita, the actress, her due, she came in person to their house to discuss the matter openly with Denise. The basic problem, according to Mum, was that Max and Rita were both artistic, impulsive, dreamers with vivid imaginations and inveterate risk takers and Denise, being mostly the opposite in personality, had become too staid and boring for him. In the end, Max and Rita went to live together until Denise finally agreed to divorce him. They had to go through a civil ceremony and be content to marry in a secular way which the state recognized as valid. Most people in our community were Roman Catholics which meant that Max and Rita could never have married in the church. Fortunately, there were no children involved so the situation was not as serious has it could have been.

Mother also gave what proved to be sound advice to a couple who were grandparents caught up in a custody battle for their grandchildren. The husband's young wife tragically died prematurely of a rare, serious illness. Naturally, the now widower, although still grieving, was looking ahead as a family man who needed a new wife and mother for his children. He'd already become friends with another young woman in our neighbourhood so he wished to re-marry before too long. His children were both girls but the younger daughter wanted to live with the grandparents whereas the elder one was much more accepting of his new wife-to-be.

With mother's guidance a satisfactory solution was worked out and later I learned that little Paulette was formally adopted by her grandparents with regular access to her father and his new family.

"Your Mother would certainly be in demand as a counsellor these days! Right you are, Marie," Doreen commented. "Talk about being born in the wrong age! She could well have had a regular column in a popular women's magazine or even develop a career as a TV celeb like a European or British version of Ophra Wimfrey!"

The five friends were becoming ever more excited and intrigued by Marie's story, being by now convinced that the book would sell successfully, thus being a guaranteed, effective fund raiser to help save Torr Brookdale Social Club from closure. Marie was about to resume her narrative of her further experiences in the period leading up to the Second World War, when Gloria called with the good news that "our funding negotiators," Bob Silverwaters and Martin Williamson (club treasurer and manager respectively) had secured a first instance project grant from a local Torr Brookdale firm, a thriving haulage business who were securing lucrative contracts over a wide area, branching out over most of Greater Manchester, as well as North Cheshire and Derbyshire. The grant would certainly cover printing and publishing costs so Rosemary would just do the proof-reading instead of the laborious, time-consuming task of typing the whole story. Rosemary said she much enjoyed the prospect of proof-reading Marie's book as it was not only very interesting it would save money needed to employ a professional proof-reader.

"Magic!" Gloria exclaimed. "Well, I'll leave you to it now. Looking forward to seeing you all next Tuesday at the club for the next instalment."

Chapter 9 – Musical Experiences including a Comical One

Marie continued her story, returning to her experiences in the period leading up to the Second World War.

My mother was such a scatterbrain that I had to organise the housework and cooking. She was also a chatterbox, which meant she often ran behind schedule with her dressmaking assignments despite having help from father as well as me in running our home. My father always managed to raise laughs all round when he used to take mother off in gushing, genteel tones when she mentioned in detail old friends from way back whom she'd met by chance when shopping or stopping for coffee at one of the numerous cafes` in the city centre.

Apart from my domestic duties and feelings of great relief when my parents had finally cleared off their debts, music and dancing played a major part in my recreation. My love of music was nurtured by joining the choir at school where the nuns taught us choral singing, mainly church pieces, to an ambitious level. The local branch of the Flemish Art, Culture and Music Movement (closely allied to the Nationalist one) included a choir and the Antwerp Music Society in turn, linked up with the Antwerp Symphony Orchestra which achieved considerable success throughout Western Europe. Occasionally guest conductors from Denmark, Holland and even parts of Eastern Europe, including Poland and Czechoslovakia, used to conduct both the symphony and concert orchestras of Antwerp. Culturally, Belgium, in common with Holland and Luxembourg, had struggled to maintain their individual identities, being often dominated by neighbouring nations. In this part of Europe these were France and Germany. Some of our composers were little known outside Belgium. Other emigrated and achieved fame on a larger cultural scale in France, Germany and the USA. Some of our musicians and composers became so closely associated with the countries to which they'd emigrated that, unpatriotically, the music and culture of their adopted countries dominated their new musical compositions. However, fortunately a number of their colleagues who stayed in Belgium, carried on Flandria's musical culture as composers, conductors, professional musicians and tutors.

Jeff Van Hove was one of these loyal colleagues. He was a prominent composer of Flemish classical and folk music as well as being the conductor of our city's symphony orchestra. He was a larger-than-life character so we all experienced some exciting times when our concerts were broadcast on Radio Antwerp. Jeff Van Hove was the Flemish Toscanini (famous Italian conductor in the 1940's and 50's). He was passionate, excitable, ebullient, sometimes moody and temperamental but he always rewarded real talent and genuine effort, so, our choir and orchestra were happy to make allowances for occasionally fraught sessions. I admired him because, amongst his other good qualities, he certainly ensured that Flemish culture was always included on local radio, cinema and the rest of the musical entertainment scene.

We enjoyed the music of the period greatly. Among our favourites were Tino Rossi, a folk singer from the Pyrenees, very popular on the continent in the 1930's and 40's, a dark haired lady from Sweden with a deep voice called Sara Leander, Fernandel, comedian and entertainer from the region in the south of France known as the Midi, Marta Eggart and Yancke Pura, soprano and tenor, Hungarian and Polish, respectively, who often played main romantic roles in the popular operettas of the day. We also enjoyed the performances of Maurice Chevalier (French entertainer) and Grace Moore, a glamorous American soprano, both very popular in those days.

The fantastic dreams you have when young! I would have liked to have performed one of the main roles in a musical show or operetta as, say it myself, I'd a good mezzo-soprano voice, having gained experience in the school choir and later in the Radio Antwerp one, enjoyed it so much but, unfortunately, I couldn't act well to save my life so that ambition was soon ended. When I was between boyfriends, having finished for good with Hendrik, there was always cousin Roger to fall back on. Now I've a very amusing incident to tell you all about. One date I went with him on was to our opera house where he'd received complimentary tickets via our music society for his excellent attendance record. The tickets were for Wagner's opera, "Lohengrin." Neither of us had been to a performance of a Wagner opera before so we thought we'd give it a go. Most of Wagner's operas tend to be rather long-winded and the wedding scene in Lohengrin was no exception – pretty long and drawn out. Roger and I wondered whether this wedding ceremony would finish by midnight at the rate it was going on. We started to get bored. Everyone in the audience around us seemed solemn, very stuffy and pompous. They looked as though their sense of humour had deserted them.

Roger brought out some gingerbread Santas – it was the feast of St Nicolas, not far off Christmas. This feast is a public holiday in Belgium. He started playing with them, dropping them on the arms of the nearest seat and then enacted, in whispered tones a comical version of the most dramatic scene in the opera so far. I could hardly stop myself from laughing out loud, so I kept desperately putting my hand over my mouth. When a couple of the gingerbread men were accidently dropped, falling into the lap of another nearby member of the audience we were nearly thrown out of the place. The usher cum programme seller made a most convincing show of giving us a good dressing down within close earshot of two stern-faced Wagner fans so we obviously were red-faced, embarrassed and felt humiliated.

However, we learned better news when he led us to the exit. In the foyer, his stern set features relaxed, the usher winked at us, explaining that he'd never been keen on Wagner and he said that he respected us for at least being honest about not liking it much, rather than pretending to enjoy the performance just for the sake of cultural snobbery. Anyway, during that same Christmas, Max, Roger's eldest brother, who heard about our memorable night out, re-enacted a comical version of a well-known Wagner opera when he invited us to their home and consequently had us in fits of uncontrollable laughter. It was a wonderful fun night out.

"I agree with that theatre usher," Doreen remarked ruefully. "I don't like Wagner either."

"I don't think any of us do," Bill added. "Wasn't he Hitler's favourite composer?"

"Yes, you're right", replied Freda. "My father mentioned this fact once. Ah, well, say no more," she finished, pulling a face which displayed much distaste.

It was another week before the friends met up again, this time at Gloria's house, one of those pleasant one-off occasions when Gloria could spare enough time to invite them all.

Chapter 10 – An Uncertain Future

Gloria was delighted that she had invited all the friends together to her home for the next instalment of Marie's most interesting life story of past times. She was pleased that it would be recorded for posterity as well as having great potential as an effective way to raise funds to keep their social club out of financial trouble and remove the threat of closure. They were now much encouraged by successfully securing the grant towards the cost of their literary project.

Norman Redesdale, the local vicar, who regularly attended Torr Brookdale community centre's meetings, was very pleased that once again the power of prayer proved to be an effective tool when any serious problem arose or adverse circumstances prevailed which seemed impossible to overcome. Even Bill, the most skeptical member of the friend's group who was inclined to be agnostic as regards any religious faith, had to admit that, on occasion, the Christian one could well be worth some consideration in future.

After enjoying Gloria's tasty refreshments and superior cups of tea, Marie gave a short re-cap of the story before and up to the point where she'd reached at their previous meeting.

"During the temporary interlude between my romances, after breaking off my engagement to Hendrik, my family and I then had rather a shock, although, looking back, we shouldn't have been so surprised given the pro-Fascist views he held. It emerged via the local grapevine that Hendrik greatly admired Hitler and, if the possibility of war became a reality, he would join the Nazis and fight on their side. Indeed, shortly after the invasion of our country started, by chance we saw him in the uniform of the Waffen-SS. He'd joined them when the occupation was imminent. If I had married him I would have ended up in a most unenviable situation when our country was liberated at the end of the war. I'd have been the widow of an SS man, as Hendrik was killed in action during the battle of Stalingrad. Branded a collaborator and my own guilty conscience to contend with life would make life not worth living after the war had ended. If I'd also had a child in tow as well, this did not bear thinking about. A mother or not, I would've felt forced to leave my country and set up a completely new identity elsewhere. Only my mother, if she'd have survived the war, the relatives with whom I was involved the most, and my closest friends, could have been trusted to keep my identity a secret. I'd probably never see them ever again. God knows where I'd have ended up. Thank God I'd had the sense to end our relationship!

The year 1939 was a very anxious time for us and our neighbouring countries. Right thinking, ordinary, decent folk whether Flemings or Walloons, thought that Hitler was, to say the least, a dodgy leader who should be prevented by some form of international legal action from being aggressive towards his neighbours to the east of Germany and his racial and political persecution of minorities in Germany and neighbouring Austria, which he'd annexed to include into the extended Third Reich. This view prevailed even more when alarming stories of Jewish and other anti-Nazi refugees' experiences of the Hitler regime came to light. Many of us had the nasty feeling that the Nazis would turn their forces onto Poland, having been handed Austria and Czechoslovakia on a plate by dithery Western European leaders who appeared to be appeasing Hitler, due either to fear or corrupt motives, most likely a combination of both, knowing the prevailing generally low opinion of politicians.

Some people, my father included, thought that if Hitler had more power in Europe they would find a natural ally to champion the Flemish Nationalist cause, having been given much encouragement by the movement winning the battle for Flemish as the official language of government, commerce and justice in Flandria. Another relevant factor was the collapse of the Franco-Belgian alliance through inter-party quarrels and disagreements. Fascist infiltration of government rendered it dangerously unstable. This factor caused our government to fail in securing any one party a sufficient majority to rule our country. The Rexist Movement, a pro-Fascist, pro-monarchist party was soon identified as the culprit. Anyway, some Flandrians thought that a strong leader who would protect Flemish civil rights and interests was what our country needed and, if the price to be paid was being friendly towards Hitler, then so be it. In politics and government, they reasoned, it was sometimes common sense to ditch some of your principles and compromise to gain the results you wanted. These very right-wing thinkers just did not realise what an evil force Nazism would prove to be – with hindsight I'm sure all but the most wicked amongst them would have abandoned it.

Although our neutrality was officially declared by our new king, Leopold the Third, France and Belgium were vulnerable to the same dangers, being so close geographically. As mother and our friends so rightly said, it wouldn't be long before Germany's aggression would unite us with France once more. We were not immediately dragged into the war, as we managed to preserve our neutrality for a while but no one was under any illusion that it would last for more than a few months. The country had been troubled for some time. An uneasy atmosphere prevailed though many young people like me were used to living for the moment and not being too concerned about the future. Antwerp was like a glittering, rosy, sapphire and gold mosaic of illuminations by night. We still enjoyed ourselves, going dancing and to theatres and cinemas, especially the latter. Apart from French favourites like Maurice Chevalier and Charles Boyer, American film stars started to grace our screens. Clark Gable was one of my favourite screen heart throbs and later, after the war, the British film actors, Stewart Granger and Laurence Olivier I found most attractive.

"Yes, those three were my mother's favourites as well," commented Freda. "It's truly remarkable when you come to think of it – film stars like sports celebs are good ambassadors for international culture and understanding between nations – they cross national barriers globally in no time!"

"Yes, Freda you're absolutely right about that", replied Marie. "Of course we also enjoyed watching films from our neighbouring countries. A film company called Uffa Fox from Germany produced some good ones but, unfortunately, as the 1930's progressed, there was an increasing amount of Nazi propaganda finding its way into the European film industry. However, our world was a pleasure cruise of city gaiety, music and bright lights but was somehow an unreal world from which I and many others were to have a rude awakening."

Chapter 11 – Invasion & More Challenges

Marie continued as usual with her story.

I'll never forget my 21st birthday on 9th May 1940 when my father held me close because I was terrified, cowering in our cellar while a massive air raid raged overhead with a thunderous crashing of exploding bombs. There had been no formal declaration of war but, at dawn that day the Luftwaffe destroyed all our aircraft that were grounded. Although our army was at full strength, it was defeated in less than three weeks when 9,000 of our troops perished during an unbroken retreat. It was certainly a disastrous time."

"I bet!" both Freda and Bill exclaimed.

"I was only four-and-a-half when the Second World War ended," Freda continued, "so, I don't remember anything of that time but my parents often said that, despite some privations here in Britain, we were truly blessed in not being invaded and occupied."

"Apart from the Channel Islands," Rosemary chimed in. "For them it must have been the most scary time in living memory. Anyway we mustn't interrupt you again. It's a most interesting and exciting story which we're all privileged to hear first hand."

On the eve of capitulation, our army made a courageous but futile attempt to stand firm in defence of our nation. However, the shock of sudden attack by an all-too-powerful enemy with its vastly superior equipment and war machine with the latest military technology was too much for us. In modern warfare it had become apparent that a small nation could not defend itself alone. Its forces would need to be united with those of an alliance of larger, more powerful states.

Our immediate anxiety fortunately was not whether food supplies would run out as Belgian agriculture had been transformed since the last war. Farmers had wisely switched to more grain and cereal growing when the international situation grew more ominous, war then becoming a strong possibility. Therefore, we, as a nation had a good reserve food supply to cover any national emergency or disaster.

What bothered mother and I was the political instability in the country thus creating a volatile situation which would be a recipe for civil war. We both wondered what would become of father as the government had fled the country to England and King Leopold had signed the infamous surrender document. Our king then made the decision to abandon our alliance with France when it became impossible to maintain, He had defended and ensured that Flemish civil rights, language and culture were protected in spite of considerable opposition from the French speaking lobby. Instead of fleeing and consequently returning to pronounce judgment on our people, who had no choice but to remain in Belgium and suffer in the occupation , he stayed with us to give us all moral support. Was this a brave act of solidarity with his people or openly supporting collaboration? My generation argued vehemently about this for the next two decades, following on from the war. I took the solidarity view as I did admire the king's courage in what must have been a terrible dilemma .

My parents separated for the second time, not long after my 21st birthday. As it happened, this did not make much difference to us as my father was expatriated, along with many others, by the Germans, in order to work for them in various parts of the Reich, including the countries they now occupied. As father was a skilled carpenter he was employed making office furniture for some Wehrmacht depots. He was later sent to Smolensk in Soviet Russia. A few years later, we learned that he was over-awed by the vastness of the country particularly the great expanse of forests which would naturally produce much good quality wood. The local people did not seem to make much use of this valuable resource except for firewood. Their furniture was very crude. Altogether, father thought they were a most primitive lot. He could not resist the urge to show them how to make furniture which was attractive as well as functional. He had a language barrier to tackle. He managed by body language, plus teaching them some basic Flemish, so they could communicate with him at least at primary school level, and worked in with informal tutorials on carpentry. He was rewarded by good quality timber being gradually converted into reasonable standard furnishings, worthy of any self-respecting apprentice.

We never heard anything of his whereabouts until nearly the end of the war when we heard he'd found himself another woman and had gone to live with her in Ghent. Thankfully, I heard this through new friends with whom I was lodging after mother's death. My friends were very reluctant to divulge this information but father was asking to talk to me to explain why he'd acted towards mother in what appeared to be a selfish way. Thankfully, was the operative word here as by now she was with the Lord and thus at peace. Had she been alive then she'd have suffered even more if she'd heard this news. Our wartime experiences and the effects of her stormy marriage had contributed to her dodgy heart condition. Yet another emotional shock would have been too much to bear. A kind, generous and courageous Christian lady like my mother did not deserve such a rotten deal as this.

When we met up father had the nerve to tell me he'd always loved her in his way. Yes, I thought, that's real rich, you left her twice in less than 25 years, remember. He said he'd been bowled over in the early years of their relationship by her exciting personality, but he maintained that it would have suited him better to have someone more grateful for his practical support and more dependant on him. He also would have preferred a wife who'd been more keen on sex. Although mother had sometimes flirted, even in early marriage and was an out-going party lover, her short skirts, sometimes daring neck lines on her blouses, high heeled shoes and regular face make-up, belied her straight-laced prim and proper sense of morality and lack of interest in the physical side of married life. By this time I was more understanding of human relationships, having had more varied experience of life, so I was not as judgmental of him as I may have been in the past. However he never meant as much to me as mother and knew he never would.

I only saw him once more before he died. This was when I was living here in England, if you please, when he asked me to support him in obtaining British citizenship and finding employment here. Talk about brazen! His political views had fortunately changed after he'd seen the results of occupation and heard about the horrendous experiences of other nations in Nazi-occupied Europe, but he nevertheless hadn't minded too much about working for the Germans. If the war had come up in conversation as it inevitably would, being still so fresh in everyone's minds, someone here could easily have reached the wrong conclusion that father was a collaborator instead of the truth, namely that he was forcibly expatriated. Father's command of English was also not as good as mine. It wasn't as if everything was still so grim back in Belgium as life was rapidly returning to normal with every sign of being more stable than ever before in its chequered history. Therefore, I pointed all this out to him and told him I'd decided not to back him up.

"We can all see your point clearly," remarked Freda "It wouldn't have been easy for him, being well into middle age, trying to cope with a new language and way of life."

"Did everything turn out all right then?" asked Bill, voicing the others' curiousity.

"Actually," Marie continued, "he never came back into England and, a few years later, I learned he'd died of a severe stroke. This was again through my friends in Belgium who also said it was a swift one so, fortunately, he didn't suffer for long."

Chapter 12 – Coping with the Occupation

To continue with my story: The next couple of chapters cover my experiences during my country's occupation by the Nazis.

Anyone who hasn't experienced their country being taken over by hostile forces who use your country as a base for their imperialistic ambitions does not realise how fortunate they have been. From all reports, it was tough enough in Britain what with bombing of several of your main cities, families split up, young men on active service daily risking their lives, girlfriends and wives wondering anxiously if their fiancés` or husbands would survive the war, rationing, etc but in Belgian and other Nazi-occupied countries it felt most devastating, demeaning and frightening. Occupation meant a loss of national morale and self-respect, a sense of total lack of control over our lives and both foreboding and feelings of hopelessness regarding the future. It created an atmosphere of distrust; the frequent fear of that knock on the door by members of the occupying force if you played even the smallest part in helping a victim of Nazi persecution or gave a modicum of encouragement to a Resistance member or anyone who'd fallen foul of the evil authority that spared no one any mercy. You could not risk making any new friends because of feeling unable to trust anyone you did not know very well. You had to be careful what you said even in conversation with local people you'd known for years as they could so easily be intimidated into giving friends away in order to protect their families. All folk who weren't collaborators felt as though Satan had taken over our city.

As you can imagine, mother and I kept a pretty low profile. The best way was to avoid open hostility and overt resistance towards the Nazi overlords as reckless heroics of this sort would only have led to retaliation by being shot dead or deported to somewhere in the Reich for slave labour. The odds were too strongly stacked against us. Undercover resistance was the much more workable scheme other than young men and women escaping to join allied forces abroad.

Early in the occupation, both of us had a shock one day when we were casually reading our local paper, As you'll probably realise, the press was heavily censored so the paper was full of Nazi propaganda. In this particular edition mother spotted a photo of the leader of the Antwerp branch of the Flemish Nationalist Movement shaking hands on the steps of our town hall with the Reich Commissioner of Flandria, the high-ranking German officer placed by the Nazis in authority over our people. It appeared that the leader of our civil rights organization, which was set up to gain justice and equality for the Flemish population, was hoping to make a pact with the Nazis whereby our people would receive concessions both material and political if they were prepared to actively support the German war effort. In other words, collaboration. I honestly thought, having respected and admired this man in the past, that he was under pressure from the Nazis to carry out their orders and had little choice but to do as they asked in order to protect us from their harsh reprisals like executions by shootings or hangings or deportations for forced labour.

"Surely," I said to Mother, "he would not actively assist the Germans by deliberately pursuing policies which are supportive of theirs?"

Mother replied without hesitation, "He's obviously become an even more fanatical Flemish Nationalist who'd make a pact with the Devil himself if he thought it would help the Flemish cause. As far as I'm concerned, I want nothing to do with people or organizations who collaborate with those horrible Nazis. If that's an example of the way our Movement operates these days, they can all take a run and jump, preferably off Mont Blanc or the Matterhorn because I'll never support them any more!" Brave words indeed! Knowing my mother, had she been younger she most likely would have joined the Belgian Resistance. As for me, although I'd no particular liking for the Nazis, I did not consider the Belgian State worth risking my life for as it had treated us Flandrians as second class citizens for years until Flanders had become more prosperous, so it could no longer ignore our Movement. Like so many of us Belgians, I'd never had a very strong sense of national identity and patriotism tended to be regional rather than national. In common with some of our people I did not realise, until the occupation had began to bite, how evil they really were.

Chapter 13 – A Poignant Tale

Soon after the Nazis had taken over our country they started rounding up the Jewish population for deportation. With all the shocks we'd had, one after another, we'd almost forgotten about our Jewish friends, the Szwarvs. We hadn't seen or heard anything of them so mother assumed they'd gone into hiding.

However, one day Martha came to visit us alone. She was in a state of utter distress. They'd split up and her daughters were being hidden by one of her other friends. She wanted to shelter in our attic or cellar for a couple of nights and was also hoping that I could take her suitcase to the railway station. A pair of friends had another suitcase and would turn up on another day at a different station between Antwerp and Bruges. As with the other friends, a Resistance contact would meet me near the next station at a pre-arranged destination where each suitcase would be handed over. Martha rightly said that she and other Jews would be too conspicuous carrying their own cases. At peak travel times Martha would mingle with the crowds and, on reaching their arrival point, for a price, a small-time crook, a loveable rogue type like an Antwerpian Arthur Daley, would issue them with false passports and fake accompanying papers.

The ultimate goal was to escape to unoccupied France and from there, into French Switzerland and, eventually by a roundabout route, to safety in either Britain or America. The suitcase plan was a clever ploy. Natives of Antwerp or Bruges, just travelling to visit friends or relatives, would not likely arouse the suspicion of the authorities provided it was planned so that not too many people would turn up with suitcases in the same place at similar times, thus attracting unwelcome attention. Their contact would ensure that they would not arrive in a strange country as destitute refugees and so, possessing some money and personal belongings would help them make their new start more easily. The network would also find money in the cases with which to bribe any officials to "turn a blind eye" along the way.

Having finalized the essential details of their escape, Martha's composure completely broke down. Heart-rending reality at facing the strong possibility of never seeing her girls again, all of them either being shot or sent to Germany or another part of the extended Reich for slave labour plus an indefinable foreboding, a sense of some fate, as yet intangible but even more horrendous paraded on her mind – who could cope with all that without becoming distraught at some point? Mother and I did our best to comfort her. All of a sudden Martha pulled herself together. Her next words re-affirmed her courage and what a fine woman she really was. Even if the Nazis captured her they certainly wouldn't find it easy to break her spirit.

"It's not really for myself I fear the most. After all I've had a good life up to recent times. I'm middle-aged and prepared to take my chance of escape on my own.

I'd much rather be captured myself. They can take me and do their worst as long as I know before then that my girls are on their way to safety. That's all the re-assurance and peace of mind I'll need. They're so young and full of zest for life so it's grossly unfair that they should have their lives cruelly ended when they've never done anyone any harm."

"Phew, could any situation be more frightening and horrific.!" Doreen expressed exactly the sentiments of all the five friends and Gloria.

"It certainly puts into perspective any problems we've ever had to deal with," Bill added. "How did you manage with the escape plan?"

Marie continued: I managed to carry out the suitcase routine although obviously nervous and on edge. I arrived at the station bright and early, just at the time when you would mingle with the crowds going to work. My contact was well chosen – a small, ordinary-looking chap with light brown mousy hair and spectacles, the sort who wouldn't easily be spotted in a crowd. Beneath my calm exterior I was scared and apprehensive throughout the whole procedure. I was more than relieved when I was finally back on the train to home. Although, on this occasion I hadn't time or opportunity to admire the beautiful medieval city of Bruges. I knew it still looked the same despite the presence of enemy alien militia. However, to me it gave the place a new menacing atmosphere, totally foreign to its usual friendly, easy-going character. I was not alone in wishing to remember it as it was before the occupation. The sun bathed the ancient brick and crenellated stonework of its historic buildings in a golden glow. In spring the tight buds on the trees lining the avenues and enhancing the canal banks, burst into fresh, bright greenery and colourful spring blossoms, casting delicate reflections on the mirror-like surfaces of the water. In summer its buildings glinted gold. In autumn, deep russet. The shadows of light and shade produced various colours , pink quartz, light copper, gentle green of ancient moss and willow trees, its neat window boxes on the terraces filled with flowers of many rich hues. In spring and summer it would be bustling with holidaymakers and weekend visitors enjoying boat trips on the canals. The prevailing atmosphere during the occupation seemed decidedly wintry.

Back home that night we heard a couple of knocks at our door. Talk about my feeling nervous, that was the century's understatement! I couldn't imagine ever feeling so scared in my entire life. Trembling, heart pounding, mouth feeling dry as sandpaper. The population were often warned that when occupying forces, chiefly the Waffen SS were rounding up Jews, Communists and all other suspected anti-Nazis that, if you were caught harbouring anyone in these categories , you'd surely be shot or deported for forced labour. The latter fate was more likely if you were young and healthy. When we both went to the door simultaneously and found that the caller was only our neighbour who asked us whether we had a small food item to spare as she'd run out of it, our relief was so overwhelming that it was akin to being rescued after a shipwreck where we'd been clinging to some rocks amidst turbulent seas with death being almost a certainty. By our reaction, she'd already guessed correctly what had been happening in our house but she was a lifelong friend of mother's and was both loyal and trustworthy. We owed her a tremendous debt of gratitude for not giving us away.

I fervently wish I could report a happy ending to this story. Tragically, I cannot do so. The girls were caught in Vichy (unoccupied France) trying to catch a train into the French zone of Switzerland. Martha gave herself up, allowing herself to be captured in the vain hope that the girls were on their way to safety and had already reached Switzerland where their contact would smuggle them across Western Europe, ultimately to Britain. It was sometimes the case that Jews who had money to spare would pay the Nazis certain amounts on the strength of their captors promising that their loved ones would remain alive if these payments were kept up. More often than not, the Nazis had no intention of keeping to their side in these agreements and so the Jew's relatives or close friends would most likely be dead or close to death in a notorious Nazi concentration camp. Word was delivered, through a grapevine of survivors rescued by the Allied Forces, some of whom turned up in Antwerp after the war ended, that Martha and the girls had perished in Auschwitz. This news arrived at a time when, fortunately, I was over the worst experiences I'd had in the war and had "turned a corner", having built a new, better life for myself with a job I enjoyed, a new home, new friends and brighter future prospects all round.

Nevertheless it depressed me for a few weeks and I felt grateful that my mother, by then deceased, had not lived to hear such terrible news. If Nazi Germany and her allies had won the war, as my mother rightly said, there'd be no point in retaining any religious faith in a benevolent God, Christian or otherwise. Thank God they were defeated.

Chapter 14 – A Wartime Romance

At the friends' next meeting, Marie re-capped regarding the war scene and her experiences in the second half of her country's occupation, gradually up to liberation, the end of the war, and the post-war scene.

Apart from occasional food shortages, the most inconvenient being bread, potatoes, meat and sugar, the unreal, tense and occasionally menacing atmosphere in which we survived from one day to the next as best we could, life was just about tolerable. For me, it began to be much more than just tolerable when I met someone, quite by chance, on a train journey to visit my blind aunt Louise at St Nicklaus. He was a most attractive young man of French extraction, although his mother was a Flandrian and they had acquired Belgian nationality. His name was Marc Champileau. He was amusing and intelligent with an air of worldly sophistication about him. He was also a witty and interesting conversationalist. Like Hendrik, he was tall and fair-haired but there the resemblance ended. Marc's face was, to my mind, more handsome and appealing. Unlike Hendrik, he had a broader outlook on life, was much more liberal minded and, when I came to know him better, not in the least possessive. I'd ample freedom to express my individuality. Marc ensured I had time to myself to spend either with friends or alone as I wished.

As you've probably gathered, Belgium like Britain and the USA, especially in the cities, was home to many different people. Over the centuries, refugees from many different countries, who fled from political, racial or religious persecution, made their permanent home there. Marc was half-French. His father's ancestors, right up to his father's time, owned a fairly large estate in Central France. Marc's ancestors narrowly escaped Madame La Guillotine during the revolution of 1789-1795 by fleeing to Belgium where at least two of his forefathers fought against Napoleon's forces. When they returned to France, they found their estate devastated and completely run down by the effects of revolution and defeat in war, so naturally it took a long time to rebuild and restore it to its former elegant, prosperous state. It never fully recovered its former glory as a couple of generations during the 19th century accumulated gambling debts so the estate was mortgaged until the eldest son of the late 19th century generation married a wealthy heiress whose father was a prominent industrialist. The First World War finally sounded the estate's death knell as the agricultural land was severely damaged and laid to waste. By then, Marc's father had married a Flemish girl and inherited a small but lucrative market garden near Antwerp. He, therefore, decided that it was more worthwhile to settle in Antwerp as, here was a sound business which, in his opinion, was a much safer investment for the future, more capable of providing financial security for his family than their doomed estate. His father proved to be right. Their business prospered until they were one of the leading market gardens in the city, supplying also the smaller towns and villages for nearly twenty miles around Flanders.

Marc and his younger brother would, between them, inherit all this one day. Naturally, Marc, being the elder son, would inherit the larger share of the business. Mum's relatives and friends were most approving and thought I'd do very well for myself if my romance with Marc ended with a marriage proposal. For me to become Madame Champileau was indeed to become Somebody, especially with Marc's aristocratic connection, be it only a relatively minor one. I'd also have financial security for life and for any children Marc and I would have. The only one who seemed to have any doubts about Marc was-yes you've guessed – my mother. I couldn't imagine how she could possibly doubt Marc's intentions. Apparently, she thought he was too much of a smooth-talking charmer. The Gallic savoir faire was responsible for his having a string of girl-friends before me. He was older than I, nearly twenty-eight, and more experienced in conducting courtships and forming intimate relationships.

Mother and I had an heated argument when my relationship with Marc was progressing well. He was originally going to get engaged to his former girlfriend (the one before me) but they broke up, having had a couple of disagreements. I also knew Marc's ex-girlfriend by sight because one of my cousins pointed her out to me once on a trip to the coast. She looked similar in appearance to me except that she was prettier, taller and looked sophisticated. She worked in one of the local banks as a clerk-receptionist . Generally she was more out-going and confident than I.

Be that as it may, I accused mother of being too suspicious minded. After all, it had been over between his ex-girlfriend and him for at least six months before he started dating me. Marc was certainly not the only one who'd attracted and dated umpteen girls. They often made better husbands when they finally settled down because they'd had more experience of the opposite sex, had enjoyed more carefree fun and excitement so they wouldn't hanker after freedom like a green, naïve youth would. "Besides," I reminded Mother, tactlessly to say the least as my words were said in anger and exasperation, "Hark who's talking! You didn't exactly select the right one, did you? Apart from his earlier philandering, we don't even know where he is now."

As I've mentioned earlier in this story, father was repatriated, along with many of our men folk, to work for the Germans in different countries which they occupied. Rubbing it in like that was hitting below the belt and, looking back, I'm certainly not proud of coming out with such catty remarks. I had someone, was loved but mother had no one really close to her other than me, having lost several good friends, Martha, victim of Nazi persecution, Isabelle, who died a Resistance heroine, and Cesarine in Holland, who, like many others in enemy occupied places, was a virtual prisoner in her own country which was suffering worse than ours throughout the occupation. Understandably, she was hurt as well as angry and retorted that she instinctively felt that Marc was not genuine and, at best was on the rebound from his ex-girlfriend who, from all reports, he'd deeply loved. She added that she didn't want me ending up as second best for someone. I deserved a better deal than that.

Marc and I used to meet in a small hotel in the countryside which had a lovely garden. It produced a riot of many colours in bloom during spring and summer. There we could forget about the war and occupation and live in a world where love conquered all, just like in operetta. Our spirits soared to a rare euphoria which only those in love would experience. In those times when we were united in body, mind, spirit and emotion, I would willingly have died several deaths for just a few hours like these. At this time I felt that if I'd never love again I could live with these wonderful memories for the rest of my life. Far from missing out, I'd been one of most fortunate people who had ever lived.

"That's brilliantly expressed," Gloria commented admiringly. "You should start writing romantic fiction, Marie. I bet you'd do every bit as well as Mills and Boon."

"Yes, the settings, locations and personal appearances of the characters are well written in Mills and Boon," said Doreen. "But their stories are so predictable; boy meets girl, one of them was unlucky in love in their past so there's some inevitable misunderstandings but it all works out neatly with the couple involved marrying and living together happily ever after. Read one and you've read virtually all of them."

"I'm out of this equation," Bill concluded. It's not p.c. of course, but that's definitely women's territory. Anyway, your story is anything but tame and predictable, Marie. We all look forward to the next episode as we're very keen to discover the final outcome."

Chapter 15 – Drama & Unwelcome Events

Marie continued with her story.

Two-and-a-half years soon passed. Towards the end of this period, we visited my blind aunt who was one of my mother's elder sisters and she was also cousin Roger's Mum. Marc joined me there but couldn't stay with me on this occasion for the full time I'd planned as he had to deliver some flowers and fruit at short notice – demands of his business sometimes encroached on our social life so I accepted this without question. I asked Aunt Louise her opinion of Marc. Up to this time I hadn't bothered about other peoples' opinion of him as he was so universally well liked and never, to my knowledge, had any dispute or disagreement with anyone apart from his former girlfriend. However, we'd been going out and otherwise spending regular time together for a long time so I now began to wonder when he'd "pop the question". It crossed my mind, of course, that the reason for Marc's delay in proposing marriage was due to the war and occupation which rendered life changing future plans a daunting and risky business.

However, in our case, I reasoned, there was no point in waiting any longer to marry as Marc had plenty of financial security and was one of the few fortunate people in steady employment without fear of collaboration accusations and possible legal charges by the Allied Powers after victory was finally achieved. After all, what could be more innocuous than the market gardening trade? Everyone needs fruit and vegetables for a balanced diet. Most people occasionally need plants and flowers to be providers of colour and beauty to brighten their surroundings, especially during the grey months of winter. Wartime and occupation only made these items more precious, expensive and often difficult to regularly obtain, but the demand was still there amongst the citizens and occupying forces alike. It was also becoming clearer, through our secret radio listening sessions broadcasted by the BBC, that, in another year or two we would likely be liberated.

These thoughts would have been going through Aunt Louise's mind as she also couldn't understand why he should not propose to me soon. However, she said that, like my Mum, she thought Marc was generally too flippant and treated some important subjects in life with an almost amoral complacency. He seemed unconcerned about injustice, oppression and brutality all of which there was a great deal in enemy-occupied Europe. She speculated that Marc could be the type who would string someone along if it suited his plans. Naturally, this was not what I wanted to hear. I was as capable as the next person for rationalising and making excuses to avoid the truth if it might be unpleasant or unlikely to work in my favour.

A couple of weeks later these matters reached a dramatic climax. I arranged to meet Marc at our usual retreat one day in mid-afternoon. To get there I used the train as it was more convenient than the tram for this destination, being only a short walk from the nearest railway station, en route. On arrival at Antwerp Central Station, I saw Marc there looking especially alert and expectant, clearly waiting for someone. From being somewhat startled at seeing him here when he was supposed to be waiting for me at Liss-Wege, near Bruges and about to ask him why the sudden change of plan without any notice, my next reaction was one of shock. Guess who turned up – his former girlfriend. Although I'd only seen her around town occasionally over the past year or so, I knew that willowy, model-like figure in its well- tailored suits, her oval face immaculately made-up, ash blonde hair in a neat perm, anywhere, even from a distance. She worked as a clerk-cum-receptionist in one of our city banks. As I looked at her I found it hard to believe that there was still a war on and our country was Nazi occupied as she had the appearance of sheer affluence. I positioned myself carefully behind a telephone booth where I could see them without their noticing me.

What I saw distressed me beyond words. They were embracing passionately and indulging in long, lingering kisses. When they departed arms linked, I felt devastated and betrayed. On the next day I was not looking forward to the showdown which would surely follow this most unwelcome development. All the same I felt I needed to confront him. When I did, he tried to evade the issue.

"I saw you with your old flame at our city station on the very day you were supposed to meet at our retreat and you didn't even have the guts to tell me to my face that, after all, I'm not the right girl for you so it's best for us both if we end our relationship!"

Marc replied that I'd no need to take that attitude as it was surely better to discover beforehand whether you both were compatible with each other for marriage than end up in an unhappy one. He said that the last two years had been a delightful episode in his life and he would look back on the period he'd courted me as a really happy experience. It was just that he thought his feelings for me weren't strong enough to survive marriage which was, for respectable, middle-class people, a lifetime commitment. As Roman Catholics, our position here was re-enforced even more.

I retorted with "What attitude do you expect me to take? You've wasted two-and-a-half years of my life, giving me false hopes of a future together. I honestly loved you and still do. It's hardly the right outcome when I've been prepared for you to propose and was so looking forward to our being happily married. I trusted you! This is how you repay me – deceit and complete betrayal of trust to crown it all!" We argued some more. The gist of his prevailing state of mind was that he seemed undecided about whether he wished to marry me or let me go and take up once more with his ex-fiancee` whom he would then marry in the not-too-distant future. He finally said he'd think it over and soon let me know what decision he'd reached. In other words, Marc would choose either her or me.

Chapter 16 – The Last Two Years of War

I spent what must have been the worst weeks of my life. By the time I was due to meet with Marc to learn what his decision about us would be, and I'd reached our usual meeting place, I was so tense and anxious that if I could have been sedated or half drunk I'd have been most grateful. He chose his former girlfriend whom he declared he'd realised that he truly loved her, not me.

A couple of weeks later, the remnants of any self-respect I had left went out of the window when I saw him a few feet in front of me, going in the same direction to the chemist's shop where I was going on an errand for some medication for mother who suffered occasionally from angina. We spoke to each other, he invited me to join him in a short stroll to talk things over but despite my agreeing to this request and his seeing the pleading look in my eyes, he still decided that

Lisette, his ex-lady friend, was the one he would marry in the near future.

My mother somehow wormed all this out of me when she saw how upset I was. "For heaven's sake girl have you no pride or any self-respect? You don't wait around, agreeing to his every whim while he tramples on your feelings, tortures you with his indecision, deceives you, playing fast and loose in every way! You should march past him, nose in the air and either say in a cold, contemptuous tone 'there's no point in discussing anything further with you. Get lost, out of my life so I can make a fresh start.' Or just ignore him and clear off soon as though he wasn't there."

How often our parents make the same mistake of assuming their children are carbon copies of themselves in character and personality! How often many of them think their children want the same things out of life as they do or at least they should want the same. I just wasn't the sort of girl to act in the same way as my mother would have done as I'd never been flirtatious –

the emotional, physical and romantic aspects of male and female relationships I'd felt very deeply. I found Marc's rejection devastating. When the worst of my grief had passed (it did feel rather like a bereavement), I suffered with depression which obviously made it difficult to cope with life. If I stayed home, I felt cooped up and, after a while, wanted to go out for a change of scene and a chance to socialize. If I went out, everywhere round Antwerp reminded me of my failed relationship and, understandably, the occupation was getting people down so much that there wasn't much cheerful company to be found, so I soon wanted to return home. I felt that I needed to do something about my predicament or I'd go mad. Unfortunately, in those days there was no counseling service available. Indeed had it not been for mother's companionship and various relatives and friends sympathizing with me I probably would have gone mad.

A couple of events were soon to break this hopeless deadlock, thank God. The Germans were in full retreat from Russia so my father returned from his repatriation where he'd been working in Smolensk, making furniture for use in the Wermacht offices, as I'd mentioned earlier in this story. He certainly had some interesting tales to tell us. He could be quite a scintillating, lively narrator when he chose to regale us with them. From what he related, it struck us vividly how vast Russia was – an impression of enormous open spaces, endless forests and lakes that would take several weeks to travel from one end to their opposite one. Compared to our small, crowded country with its closely packed conurbations here in Flandria and in the Borinage, industrial heart land of Wallonia, our small city of Antwerp where many of us knew each other and, even in the countryside, you were never very far from either a railway or the coast. The contrast couldn't have been greater. It took a considerable leap of the imagination to visualize such a place.

A young Russian peasant woman who lived with her mother and her small daughter in a log cabin had befriended father. As was the case with many such humble households, her husband was missing, presumed dead. He had previously joined the Red Army and vowed he would join up with the guerilla resistance if their country was invaded by Nazi Germany. His wife knew that her husband would certainly be much displeased with her for taking in a lodger who was working for the enemy, albeit as a civilian conscript from one of the Reich's conquered countries. However, in a perilous situation such as many ordinary Russian people found themselves, finer feelings and grand moral scruples were not high priorities on their agenda – survival was the name of the game.

She seemed to find a good friend and soul mate in my father who did little favours for her and her family, which really had the personal touch. He noticed that in winter she wore a rough, basic fur coat with one hole for the head to go through and two holes for the sleeves to fit in. They were clumsily stitched onto the armholes. Anyway my father decided she wouldn't need to put up with looking like a tramp any more. He designed a stylish coat for her, cut it with real fashion flair and showed her how to sew it more tidily and professionally. He could be a very entertaining story teller and gave us many occasions to enjoy a much needed, good laugh for the first time in ages- the pair of them strutting around like a baron and baroness with her elegant, new coat, the fur coat he'd also made for himself and their designer furniture including attractive wooden toys for her small daughter that my father had made for them all.

Although keenly interested, the friends wondered when Marie would reach the end of her story. It was looking like a formidable challenge to get this book edited, printed and finally published in time for the community centre to benefit financially. Marie resumed her narrative regardless.

"Reading between the lines, it looked as though Dad had been up to his old tricks again, unable to resist having affairs with other women. In this instance, we had no way of knowing whether it had happened or not.

Therefore, mother and I dismissed it from our minds. Sometimes he was away from our house for the occasional day. Later on, around three months after our liberation in 1945, when mother by then was on her deathbed, I heard, via our city's grapevine, that when he disappeared again he was in fact living with a young woman on the east side of Antwerp, Roosendaal, not far from the Dutch frontier. It was a doomed relationship as she was expecting his child, miscarried with the shock of regular bombing over our city from both the enemy and the Allies and she was killed in the final air raids. My father was an impossible chap altogether – he possessed a charming personality, was always expert at rationalizing reasons for his infidelities and occasional tendencies to be very selfish.

As with everyone else in our country, the momentous events of history swept us along; no one was unaffected in our daily lives. The Allies were gradually making their way through Western Europe into Germany; the Russians were doing the same from the east. In the autumn of 1944, they arrived on the frontiers of the Third Reich, determined to deal the coup-de-grace` that would end the war. By way of anti-climax, my lifestyle and indeed my life was changed permanently because of these major events.

Chapter 17 – Plans to defeat the Enemy

Sometimes history does repeat itself. It certainly did in our chief waterway, the Scheldt. Back in the 16th century, the two coastal provinces, Holland and Flandria, became the main area of armed resistance against the Spanish invaders. The long, narrow strip of half submerged swampland, stretching from the Scheldt to the Dutch waterway, the Heller was captured by the Duke of Alva's Spanish army who marched at ebb tide across the ten mile channel to reach it. Courageous Flandrians and Dutch, appalled by the cruelty inflicted on their people by the Spanish invaders fought a desperate battle for several years to defeat them. The Spanish army managed to seize two more islands in 1575, despite fierce resistance and desperate measures by the Netherlands people. These islands were later recovered by the Flandrians and Dutch, Now, some 370 years later, Canadian and British troops would perform similar feats to liberate our country and our Dutch neighbours from another equally cruel invader.

Freda, Doreen, Bill, Harry, Rosemary and Gloria had, to date, followed Marie's story through copies of each week's episode via email attachments or printed photocopies when they could not all be present to hear her narrative. However, they preferred to listen in person as they were excited and intrigued by her scintillating, witty and superb story telling.

"And you said earlier on in your story that you wanted to become an opera singer or star in operettas and musicals but dismissed these dreams because you couldn't act." Gloria wagged a finger and spoke to Marie in mock disapproval. "Talk about being overly modest! The way you relate your life history, you should have been signed up with RADA years ago."

"Well, I'll have fame at last if my book plays a major role in saving our centre from closure," replied Marie "Who knows, I might even be invited to appear on a Granada TV chat show. Then I can relate my experiences of growing old disgracefully!"

"Never marginalize or dismiss senior citizens as not having anything of value to contribute to or offer society. That's my view," Freda chimed in.

"We all second your statement, Freda!" they all chorused.

"Anyway, let's recap," said Gloria "Yes, we're up to the part about history repeating itself over the liberation of Belgium and Holland."

"Moving on from that point", Marie continued, "Antwerp, our city, was, as it is today, an important port. By 1938, it had six square miles of docks which handled 60 tons of freight each day and could accommodate 1,000 ships at a time. We also had 26 miles of quays, 625 cranes, many marshalling yards, cold storage plants, coal hoists and oil tanks. Strategically, Antwerp was an ideal garrison port, despite its defences being about thirty years older in concept and design than those of the 1940's. Anyway it was most valuable to the Germans who were determined to secure it during both world wars.

Unfortunately, the odds were in their favour on both occasions. In World War One, Dutch neutrality had closed our link-up waterway, making our city an immediate target for their advance and in World War Two our army and allies were stuck in France, desperately trying to stop the Germans advancing on Sedan, an important strategic place en route into Belgium. Therefore, Antwerp fell into German hands yet again."

"While we're in the modern history mode, Marie, wasn't Antwerp chosen as the embarkation port for the German 16th army in Operation Sea Lion, the German invasion of Britain?" Bill asked.

"Yes, Bill, you're absolutely correct on that point," Marie beamed. Anyway, fortunately, as we all know this invasion failed and, especially after the Allied victory in the battle of El Alamein in 1942, the tables were more swiftly turning against Nazi Germany. As the Dutch coast was beyond the range of fighter coverage from

Britain's airfields, it was ruled out for the Allied landings, Therefore, it became vital that the Scheldt needed to be opened before too long. Then our city would play a very important part as the best strategic base from which to invade Germany and finally end the war."

Bill, who was keenly interested in World War Two commented, "I bet you were in a really frightening position at that time with the strong possibility of a major battle and bombing campaign looming ."

"Indeed we certainly were," Marie recalled, shuddering. "Our city, along with those of the coast of Northern France, was a port selected by Hitler as one of his most important fortresses as he reasoned that the Allies could not invade the Reich successfully unless they could capture a large port speedily. These coasts were then planned to hold a long line of steel and concrete structures, stretching from Bolougne all the way to Maastricht, Holland. In 1944, these fortresses, designed for defence of these coastlines and to frustrate the Allied advance, on Hitler's orders, were placed under the command of General Von Runstedt, Commander-in-Chief for occupied North Western Europe. The Fuhrer also directed that his fortresses must be held at all costs and their garrisons strengthened. To crown it all, our waterway, the Scheldt, was heavily mined and obstructed in September of that year.

Von Runstedt very much disapproved of this system. For one thing, the Germans were fighting on too many fronts, gradually accumulating more casualties and losing the war. He'd not enough men for this onerous defence task without locking large garrisons within the fortresses in order to hold then effectively. The garrisons, their commanders discovered, were too small. Control over naval and Luftwaffe units in their localities was also limited. Correctly, Von Runstedt knew the Allies wouldn't be mad enough to attack the fortresses from their front but would have to capture them landward from the rear of the fortresses. The

Allies ingeniously resolved these difficulties by designing and constructing the Mulberry Artificial Harbours which, as we all know, were most successful in the D-Day Landings, eventually liberating Europe from the Nazi tyranny."

Bill and Harry then announced enthusiastically that they would be taking a short holiday, joining a coach party to Normandy to see the Mulberry Harbours.

"It will be a very interesting conducted tour," Bill continued excitedly. "I can't wait!"

"I grant you permission to go on your boys-'only weekend," Doreen said in mock solemn tones. "On one condition. That we two will enjoy a romantic dining experience at that newly renovated country inn, advertised on local radio recently."

"Yes dear, better go easy on souvenir expenditure then. You see folks, I daren't go against *she who must be obeyed!*"

Marie cleared her throat and announced that the present session would be closed as, at their next meeting, her story would become even more exciting and interesting."

Chapter 18 – Events Leading up to Liberation

All the friends ensured they were present for Marie's next installment.

She continued: Well, the Allies did a brilliant job of capturing Antwerp but not without a heavy price paid in casualties, including the armed forces but also military and civilian workers at our docks, who supported the air forces and Bomber Command, the naval support squadron, members of the Belgian and Dutch resistance and our civilian citizens bombed by V-Weapons.

Antwerpians particularly admired the British minesweeping forces and their highly skilled divers who had to detonate mines near the quayside or lock gates, to prevent damage to vital supplies of road building materials, replacement rail track, points, signals and equipment essential to bringing our port back to normal working order. The minesweeping men were enthusiastic; thoroughly committed to their massively important and dangerous job. They also possessed great stamina. Naturally, it was most rewarding when they found a mine to diffuse as they were such a deserving work force. Long hours, tough working conditions in freezing water and mud, mostly in pitch darkness, the constant threat of bombs exploding with very little warning was, by anyone's standards, the most physically and mentally exacting, stressful job one could ever do.

We felt totally in debt to them and our gratitude was such that whenever or wherever the opportunities arose, hospitality to these and other Allied forces was a must.

We were also proud to learn that Terneuzen, the Scheldt's chief shipping pilot who'd escaped to England back in 1940, having defied and evaded enemy patrols and bombs, returned to accompany the minesweeping forces to give them practical assistance. A brave man indeed he turned out to be although previously some of our people thought he'd been cowardly in fleeing to

England while we all were enduring Nazi occupation but he was a courageous man indeed. It just shows you how quickly and easily we can pre-judge and jump to wrong conclusions about other people's characters.

Before our port was rescued and opened by Allied forces, the greatest menace to our people, our homes transport services, factories and warehouses were the dreaded V-weapons. Between October 1944 and March 1945, when bombardment ceased, 1,214 V-weapons fell on Antwerp and its suburbs. They killed around 3,000 people, and seriously injured another 12,000. More than 150 V1's and 152 V2 ballistic missiles fell in the docks, causing damage to shipping petrol tanks and installations. Fortunately, the damage was not as severe as was feared. Thanks to the fire-fighting crews, fires were swiftly extinguished. By far the worst single incident occurred a couple of weeks before Christmas 1944 when a V2 hit our Rex cinema, killing 242 military personnel and 250 civilians with a further 500 others seriously injured.

Personally, I found what was most scary about these weapons was that, when a raid started, there was firstly a rumbling noise rather like a thunderstorm beginning, followed by a high pitched whine which grew louder before the actual explosion. Sometimes they'd start up, stop and then start over again so it wasn't easy to judge when and where best to run for shelter if one was going to explode near you.

"As if you people hadn't enough to contend with, never mind those terrible bombs as well," Gloria remarked. "People must have suffered much post-traumatic stress."

"Yes, especially the more highly strung," Marie replied, shuddering. "We ordinary folk called it "nervous trouble" in those days. Some went as voluntary patients to our local mental hospital. One of my cousins worked there, helping with the rehabilitation of bomb victims. I remember there was a lovely big garden in the hospital grounds where my cousin and the patients tended regularly. It always looked a showpiece even in winter. Must have been a haven of tranquility for them. Anyway, regarding V-weapons: I had a narrow escape from them which I'll tell you about when I include it in my next three installments which cover my experiences up to leaving for England to start a new life."

The friends were unanimous in their opinion that Marie, having survived the occupation and bombing from both sides in that war, must have been grateful for every day she was alive and well thereafter.

"Yes, it's amazing what we all take for granted and sometimes are apt to get irritated over trivial matters and minor inconveniences," Rosemary commented fervently. "Despite some rough patches we all go through in life, our generation has been especially fortunate in many ways."

Chapter 19 – Liberation

The next installments Marie related to the friends covered the period from late 1944 through to February 1947 when she left Belgium to settle permanently in England.

It was during the liberation of Belgium that I sought employment at one of the Allied Army canteens which sprung up around Antwerp to cater for their troops, mainly British, American and Canadian. These brave troops arrived in great numbers to capture Antwerp and to liberate our city and the rest of the country.

Housekeeping and catering were really the only skills by which I could earn a living. My mother once had the notion that I might become a partner in her small dressmaking business which she ran from our home. However, her sewing standards were, of necessity, exacting and I could not achieve as high a standard although, I thought I wasn't too bad at it. At least I could sew by machine in a straight line and do basic repairs. Nevertheless mother always termed my sewing efforts "bits of masonry – Marie you're too ham-fisted for words!" that's why I ended up doing most of the cooking and housework while she just about kept our heads above water financially by running the business.

Quite frankly, I was rather apprehensive about starting work at age twenty-five after always being at home since leaving school.

"I bet you were," Freda said, ruefully. "Having to embark on such a drastic lifestyle change must have been quite a challenge for you."

"Yes, it was," Marie replied. The halting tone in her voice suggested a struggle to build up her self-confidence at that time.

"You see, I'd never worked for anyone other than Mum and, at that, in a sheltered environment. I'd only received payment that was little more than pocket money as the 1930's depression had hit small businesses quite hard so she could not often afford to pay me a bigger wage. I was, therefore, rather pleased at the prospect of earning a proper wage with the pride and dignity that comes with achieving this goal. It would help mother very much as she could not work at the same speed now as before owing to her failing health. She was on regular medication for her heart condition.

My self-doubt about working outside my comfort zone was caused partly by having to fit in with ordinary, working-class girls who, in those days only had a basic education by which to get by in the outside world, whereas I'd received a superior education at a private convent school and could speak basic English as well as Flemish and French. I also had a considerable knowledge of history, our country's legal system and politics. I thought that as companions, they wouldn't have much in common with me and I'd find it difficult to know what to discuss with them. They may have felt inferior to me with my middle-class background and grammatically correct, refined speech and, by way of self-defence, might make unkind fun of me.

However, I'd have to cross that bridge when I reached it because, after all, I told myself, I'd learned more intellectual material at school than some of my contemporaries, resulting in greater general knowledge but not sufficient specific knowledge and skills to earn a living . I wasn't too good at expressing myself on paper either, mainly due to not being a good speller. Therefore, I wasn't really superior to them.

The first job I applied for was at the American Servicemen's Canteen. Everyone round Antwerp was talking about what generous wages they paid and how exciting for the young women to have a dynamic, fun-loving American boyfriend who'd take them out on the town, giving them a wonderful time with parties, dancing and cinema shows. The Americans liked to spend generous amounts of money on them, sent them flowers, gave them chocolates and perfume, were more romantic than the local young men and made them feel really special.

Young women of my age group were fed up with Belgian men as they often took you for granted and expected much of you for what they offered in return. I heartily endorsed those sentiments, having been taken for a ride by Marc in the recent past.

Years later, I reflected that the young Belgian men of my generation were, in fact, a lost generation who, apart from those brave souls who joined The Resistance, felt they were condemned whatever they did. They felt morally obliged to surrender to the Germans in 1940 in order to avoid paying the heavy price in fatalities experienced during the carnage of World War I when their fathers made an heroic stand against a formidable enemy. Time, growing older and increased wisdom, albeit some gained by hindsight, made me develop a more tolerant opinion of them.

Anyhow, to return to my first introduction to the working world outside of home, I duly arrived for my interview with the manageress at the American base canteen. I was surprised to find that their manageress was a rather flashy lady with bright-red painted fingernails, lipstick to match and a short skirt, more like a night club hostess than a personnel manager for a catering services department. She wanted me to parade up and down, stressing the importance of their waitresses possessing good legs and figures because most G.I. s preferred ones who would display their natural, physical assets in this way. Now, say it myself, I'd quite a good pair of legs despite being only short in stature so they were not always seen to their best advantage. However, although no prude, I was still rather uneasy about joining their staff. I still hoped that one day I'd find that special man who would make me eager to spend the rest of my life with him but being one of a collection of sex symbols for lusty G.I.s and the obviously risky situations that might arise there did not appeal to me at all. Therefore I turned down their offer of employment.

Shortly afterwards I was relieved to land myself a

waitressing job at the British Army NAAFI canteen in the Antwerp Arms in our city centre. The British did not pay as much as the Yanks did, but I was more than compensated by the good company, happy atmosphere there and the servicemen were gentlemen, appreciating us and paying sincere compliments without being too brazen. As for my doubts about fitting in with my fellow workers and my first negative feelings about having rather come down in the world, I soon berated myself for being a fool and a snob. I was pleasantly surprised to find that, within a short time, I made a couple of good friends there.

Gloria and the friends marveled at the stamina Marie possessed for her age. She seemed able to talk non-stop for an hour or more at a stretch. Her memory was truly remarkable. Next time they all met they certainly would be eager to know about Marie's new friends at the canteen and more of her interesting experiences.

Chapter 20 – New Friends and My Narrow Escape

On this next occasion, sure enough, they all met up and Marie as usual never failed to hold the attention of her small but nevertheless enthusiastic audience.

"One of my friends was Jeanette, a girl whom my relatives and even my Mum who was no snob, would certainly not have approved. She was full of fun and laughter, effervescent with a high spirited manner, good-hearted but with a reputation for being what society called in those days "a good time girl." There were whispers among the locals that she'd sometimes earned money on the side at what they politely termed dubious means. However, she was very popular and became a special friend of mine. Despite being a few years younger than me Jeanette was modern and broad-minded enough to discuss my private concerns with.

Yvonne, another of our band, was a similar type to

Jeanette, early twenties, pretty, brunette with a bubbly personality. There the resemblance ended. Yvonne came from Wallonia and, unfortunately, was rather biased against us Flemings. Unlike Jeanette, she had snobbish inclinations, boasting that her father was a high ranking officer in the regular army who had become a resistance hero. However what Yvonne did not know was that, quite by chance, our canteen manageress, Madame Verecker, in conversation with her husband when off duty, heard that Yvonne's father was in fact just a senior executive officer in the military finance department. He'd fled to England when our country was invaded and returned to help the Resistance but at a somewhat later stage when the worst perils had ended. Paul Verecker, who had a good sense of humour, joked with Madame, " What will our Yvonne romance about next week – Mon Pere` owns a chateau in the Dordogne!"

I had good reason though, to thank Yvonne as she gave me the opportunity to become more assertive when she started an argument in which she advocated closer ties with France as she'd never liked being associated with the half-educated, rather crude Flemish country bumpkins whose loyalty to the Allied cause was questionable on many occasions. Usually timid little me saw red. I pointed out indignantly that our Head of Antwerp PublicWorks Dept, Robert Deykemans, a Flandrian, risked his life to cut through barbed wire on the main bridge near Boom which was still held by the Germans, after guiding the Allied armies through a countryside full of instillations still occupied by the enemy. This assured a clear passage through to enable the Allies to capture and liberate our city. Another Flandrian hero, Pilaet of the Belgian Resistance, escaped from Gestapo custody to actively assist the Allies to liberate Antwerp.

Flanders had also produced world famous artists such as Rubens and Van Dycke, led the country in music and literature and also kept our nation fed in both war and peacetime as Flanders had rich farmland and well managed agriculture. Wallonia with its ailing coal and steel industries would be unlikely to survive as an independent state whereas Flanders would stand a better chance to do so. Closer ties with France would also be unlikely to happen as France had never shown much interest in joining up with Wallonia in any way. I finished my opposing views by stating that she had no right to tar all Flandrians with the same brush just because a minority were undoubtedly traitors. Jeanette diffused the argument by jokingly chipping in about our country already having government and opposition representatives in our canteen of all places. She wanted to know when we'd be forming the post-war government!

On a more sober note, I experienced a narrow escape from the bombs while employed at the Antwerp Arms canteen. One momentuous day I'd good reason to thank God on my bended knees for my survival.

V-weapon bombardment began well before our port was opened. The first V2 ballistic missile hit

Antwerp on 12th October, 1944 and the first flying bomb on 23rd. In January 1945, a couple of months before I became involved with Pete Beresford, I hesitated whether to take a short cut from Provinciestraart where my home was, to catch the tram to my workplace, the British Servicemen's canteen at Minerva Motor Works which was five miles outside Antwerp. The short cut took me through a couple of back streets (rather a maze for anyone unfamiliar with the area to tackle as the streets looked similar to each other) but it saved a long walk through the main street to the tram terminus. In fact it was only 10 minutes walk opposed to nearly 25 minutes by the main route.

That particular day some sixth sense kept warning me not to take the short cut. The bombardment was gradually reducing being not as severe as it had been in the period before Christmas so I didn't see why I could not take a chance as thousands of others were exposed to the same risks. There was a battle raging in my mind between what seemed to be a psychic message or the

Holy Spirit's still, small voice and my reasoning. As a Christian I decided the former was the still small voice from the Holy Spirit. Anyway this message won so I travelled the longer way round. Later on, one of our neighbours told me that the back streets near the tram route had all their buildings blown sky high by a V2 missile. The blast was so powerful that all that was left was a row of shoes belonging to the victims who must have died instantly. Most poignantly there was a few pairs of childrens' shoes amongst the row. I contemplated the grim thought that I could easily have been among those victims on that day. Years later, living in England and hearing so much in the news media about nuclear weapons being a thousand times more powerful than even the atom bomb I decided it didn't bear thinking about for long. I'd seen and heard enough in Antwerp of the destruction wrought by the relatively humble V weapons, never mind anything worse.

Ironically sometimes we were even in danger from allied bombs being dropped by mistake when they were en route to attack E-boat bases on the western Dutch coast. The 8th US air force were accidently responsible for the bombing of a children's home situated a few miles on the eastern outskirts of Antwerp, our city being only half an hour by road from the Dutch frontier. It was indeed a tragic accident as there were no survivors. Several corpses of the nuns were found on top of the children's bodies. They had obviously been trying to protect their charges. The American air force chiefs were deeply remorseful for what had happened so they not only paid for and erected a memorial to the staff and children, they also paid for a new home to be built. There was no expense spared on the new building with more facilities for residents and staff than ever before.

Local people were of the opinion that might almost have emanated from the British in those times. They applauded the American generosity of spirit but thought these Yanks were too reckless and trigger happy with firearms for their   liking – think they can perform miracles. Too dangerous having no self doubt like that.

However, I thought that you certainly couldn't fault them on kindness, honesty or integrity in not only admitting their mistake but also doing their utmost in the circumstances to compensate the community. This showed them to be both decent and trustworthy.

Chapter 21 – Love and Romance at Our Base

Within our canteen, we all had a laugh, strictly amongst ourselves, about the peculiar food tastes of the British troops. A birthday party was held for Don, a young sergeant in the REME (Royal Electrical & Mechanical Engineers) Division, in our canteen as he'd reached his quarter century (25 years of age). As well as a comical birthday cake with a cowboy hat and gun formed in chocolate (Don's favourite reading matter was paperback Westerns) which Madame managed to obtain for free through friendship with the American base, there was a slap-up tea with salad, two different varieties of cheese, roast ham and pork pies and for dessert, some fresh fruit, jelly and blancmange, would you believe! A bit silly for a grown man to enjoy, but the way some of them carried on, with their practical jokes, friendly rivalries and clowning about, they seemed to us like overgrown schoolboys.

As for putting meat in pies, to us Belgians it appeared very odd as we'd never tasted them before. We always cooked our meat in casseroles, stews or served cooked cold meat in salads and sandwiches. Come to think of it, with wartime food shortages and rationing in so many countries as well as any national emergency situation which could arise, it wasn't such a bad idea as the meat would go further and you'd benefit from a substantial, economical meal, especially in winter.

"Yes, Marie, what you've just said takes me back to my late Mum's tales of her wartime experiences," Freda commented. "The family managed to improvise in all sorts of ways with meals. Glamorgan sausages was one that particularly stuck in my mind. They were made with dried egg, grated cheese, onions, breadcrumbs and fresh herbs from the garden. Very tasty too. Carrots were added in cakes as a substitute for dried fruit shortages. Mum even put them in a flan with lemon jelly she'd stored a few months previously."

"My aunt, now deceased, still remembered decades later the terrible coffee they used to serve in cafes` and the makeshift sort you bought in the shops," Bill laughed. "I know that chicory was added to a considerable degree but the rest of the ingredients used is a mystery to this day!"

"What you produced on allotments in those days – that is the Dig For Victory Campaign which I read about, being just a bit before my time," Gloria added, "did help no end in keeping people healthy. In fact, some food experts claim that our wartime diet was more healthy than our modern ones."

"That might be true," said Doreen. "Especially with some folk in high pressure jobs coupled with busy lifestyles, dashing about, making do with scrappy snacks and too much convenience food. Let's hope they'll realise about sensible eating before they damage their health."

"Better let you continue with your story," Harry

brought them back into the listening mode.

Marie continued. Romance was certainly in the air. Most of the girls were soon to find boyfriends and eventual husbands amongst the enormous number of foreign allied troops stationed in Antwerp. As I said earlier, disillusion with our own eligible young men, plus the excitement of being romantically involved with someone from another country and learning about new cultures and lifestyles, was something none of us cared to miss out on. In those days, most of us hadn't travelled very far. Our travel adventure highlight was usually a day trip or short holiday to the nearest seaside resort from home. Some of the British army were quite an international lot as they had, amongst their ranks, Poles, Czechoslovaks, De Gaulle's Free French, Norwegian and Danish, refugee troops who had escaped from their occupied countries to join any allied army who were fighting against the Nazis. There were some Southern Irish volunteers, too. Last but not least, a frequent visitor to our canteen was a gentleman named Franz Adolf Felix Stein, a German-Jewish refugee who'd been selected for the REME corps because of his considerable skills with vehicle maintenance and repairs.

There were many romances blossoming at our canteen. Some even managed to secure dates with Canadian troops as there were many of their divisions involved in the liberation and rehabilitation of our port and its surrounding area. Unfortunately, my pal, Jeanette's romance with a Canadian officer did not end happily as he already had a girl friend back home whom he'd promised to marry when he finally returned to Canada. He decided to honour his promise to his fiancé,` so Jeanette was left to pick up the pieces of her broken heart. Two months later, Madame and two members of staff had to administer first aid to Jeanette as she was suddenly taken ill. She was then conveyed in an ambulance to the city hospital where she was treated for miscarriage, having been nearly two months' pregnant. At least she'd been lucky enough not to have ended up an unmarried mother. Although on the continent, people had a more tolerant attitude to such a predicament than probably in Britain in those days, many still, especially older people, took a dim view of girls who ended up in this situation. As she'd no immediate family either to rally round to help her, she would have faced a lonely, uncertain future. Eventually though, everything worked out much better for Jeanette. Canteen gossip confirmed what I, as her friend, had suspected for several weeks. By now we all had the pleasure of seeing bright, cheerful and bubbly Jeanette back with us again. Jeanette had found herself a new boyfriend from among our British REME lads, an Englishman called Jeff Meakin. They were real lovebirds in no time. I can still remember the photo one of the other chaps had taken of them. Their facial expressions would certainly have made any girl or woman still searching for the right man, absolutely green with envy.

The most incongruous couple to get hitched were Yvonne and Vincent. Like Jeanette, she was very happy with her chosen partner. Vince was completely bowled over by what he termed her "dynamic Continental allure and sex appeal." The first time he saw her, I recall he exclaimed gleefully "By gum what a little cracker! Bet she's great fun to go on a date with. Never come across one like her back home!"

(Yvonne was only 5ft 2, in height even shorter than I). Vince was a blunt, forthright Yorkshire lad, rather naive and, until his wartime military service, hadn't travelled much further than his home town, so his fellow servicemen said. Yvonne must have seemed the height of glamour and sophistication to such a young man. We Flandrian peasantry grudgingly admitted that she certainly knew how to wear clothes and make the best of her appearance all round. Even in our plain utility working outfits she showed off her well proportioned, sexy figure to her best advantage. I privately thought she'd lead him a merry dance and wondered if he could trust her to remain faithful throughout their marriage. I did, however, thank her personally for almost introducing me to the man who would become my future husband.

"So she turned out to be more generously spirited than you thought," Doreen remarked. "When the chips were down we did the same to help each other in Britain. Somehow a real crisis, such as war or a major natural disaster, fortunately often seems to bring out the best in human nature."

"Yes, Doreen you're spot on there. Indirectly, it was generous of her to take an interest in me when I wasn't a close friend and held opposing political views as well."

"Zat good looking boy, Pierre 'as been asking after you zee uzzaire day, Marie. Why not let him chat you up?"

I replied, somewhat frostily. "I'm not running a kindergarten yet, Yvonne. Why, he looks only about nineteen. I'm nearly 26."

However, it was true that Peter Beresford was handsome, extremely youthful in appearance and enjoyed attempting to speak some basic Flemish so that he could manage to communicate and converse with us, putting the accent on romance. On second thoughts, I decided that I'd nothing much to lose by getting to know him at first instance as a friend as, after going on a couple of dates with one of the Irish volunteer servicemen and discovering that he wasn't the man for me, it now seemed a more worthwhile proposition. My theory proved to be correct. I was pleasantly surprised to learn that he was twenty-three and he turned out to be good company. This was the most effective cure for my heart-breaking, bitterly disappointing experience with Marc. I also realised that, coming up to my late twenties, it might be my last chance of finding a suitable man to marry.

Peter Beresford was an Englishman from Cheshire, a widow's son, and an apprentice garage mechanic before being called up for military service in 1940. His being three years younger than I was also a good ego and morale booster. I started to look forward to our dates and our relationship seemed to be developing rapidly into a full-scale romance when I received some very unwelcome news.

The friends' meeting drew to a close with the five of them and Gloria on tenterhooks until their next get-together. They all hoped that Marie's grim news was not too great a shock for her as she'd experienced considerable ill luck and traumatic episodes in her young adult life.

Chapter 22 – A Dramatic Event and a New Life for Me

Marie took up her story again at their next meeting. She opened with this statement: "It seemed as though as soon as I became in luck's way something went wrong for me, making me wonder if I'd ever turn that corner to a better future."

I received official word that my mother was arrested. When our government were newly back from exile in England they immediately started rounding up collaborators. Due to my father's general sympathy with the Fascist viewpoint before the war, Hendrik, a Fascist supporter paid frequent visits to my home when he was my boyfriend and them both being disillusioned with the Belgian State, some people must have formed the impression that my mother, too, had held the same opinions. However, local people and those in authority around Antwerp should have known better as she was well-known in our small city. Many folk must also have known that she was close friends with Martha Szarv who was a local Jewish business woman. Therefore, she was the last person to ever sympathize with the Fascist cause. This made the situation all the more alarming for me. As well as the emotional shock and fear of further damage to her already fragile health, I had to cope with anger at the injustice perpetrated by this false accusation.

I felt, in the midst of this nightmare, on visiting her in the tiny cell within the grim fortress of a jail, I thought it best to ask a couple of our relatives to give their necessary backing to clear up the mistake. I did not wish to involve Pete mainly because of the language barrier problem. He naturally hadn't mastered Flemish enough yet to be of practical help in that way. Fortunately, Cousin Roger and his family spoke up for my mother, giving convincing evidence in her favour to the government officials dealing with her case. As you can imagine, this was an immense relief to me and I was most grateful to them for securing mother's release within a couple of days. However, this distressing, humiliating experience was the last straw for her as her heart condition was worsening. A month later, she died, aged only fifty-five.

My father turned up at her deathbed. As I regarded him as partially responsible for her premature death, he received a very frosty reception from me. Life was rapidly returning to normal in Antwerp so it was no longer a matter of oppressed people practicing solidarity regularly, burying any differences of opinion, resentments or personal dislikes in order to survive. I virtually disowned him as, to my mind he'd repaid her love and loyalty with deceit and unfaithfulness. Mistakes she may have made. Who indeed hasn't? They probably were not too well suited to each other, but his conduct was still not justifiable.

I found myself being angry with God for having her life so cruelly cut short and giving her a dirty deal for many years of her lifetime, in view of her being such a friendly, caring and generous person. It was particularly poignant sorting out her relatively few possessions at our little house in Provincie-Straat. The small timber yard and shed where my father used to work at his carpentry and how, to me then as a little child, he could do magic with a dull block of wood, turning it into a work of art that was both useful and decorative. Our house, for me now, was a trip down memory lane which was sometimes happy and amusing, sometimes sad and painful but a shock that this long chapter in my life was closed forever. I knew what Pete would have said had he accompanied me on this occasion. "The past is dead – there's nothing you can do about that but you can certainly learn from any mistakes or wrong decisions you later regret making, so it does have some value after all. Best thing to do now is look to the future."

Of course he was right. To his bit of homespun philosophy I added " It takes a long time, as you go through life, to realise that you're making your past via the present all the time, so what once was the future is now the past. You can easily waste years in negative worrying, vague fears and not being honest with yourself about what you want out of life and relationships. Having unrealistic expectations about what, for you, is achievable is also a temptation that only leads to false hopes, disappointment and frustration." Pete nodded in agreement and said, "My Mum always held the view that you should never ditch your dreams as long as they're feasible and never abandon your ideals about helping to create a better, more just society. If you abandon both, you'll be much devalued as a person."

"My, we are in a profound mood tonight!" I chuckled in an attempt at welcome light-heartedness. We then hugged each other, thankful that we were still young and realising how fortunate we were to have survived the war. In fact, it was now great to be alive.

I had to act decisively soon as it was highly unlikely, even if we'd been on better terms in the relationship area, that my father would ever return to live in our old home. Indeed he'd already received a good offer of alternative accommodation from a friend which he told me he'd be a fool to turn down. There was not much to deal with regarding our house as, in common with most people in our country, we never owned the place. It was rented. Even some of our furniture was inherited from earlier tenants, with my parents taking over ownership of these unwanted items when they moved in. Home ownership was only available to wealthy people. Anyway, once I'd finally paid off the last rent installment and I was given reasonable time to pack my possessions and move out, I had to find new accommodation speedily.

The friends were now curious regarding where Marie would land and what her new landlord or landlady would be like, so they were especially looking forward to the next installment of her life story.

Chapter 23 – My New Home

Marie continued with her latest installment about her new home.

Searching round the Antwerp suburbs for a couple of furnished rooms, I spotted a notice in one house window in the large, fairly smart suburb of Edegen. Despite bomb damage, this area looked as though its appearance would soon return to normal. The family who were letting the two top rooms of their home turned out to be most friendly folk who readily agreed for me to lodge with them. They quickly made me feel like one of their family, rather than just a lodger. Apart from my canteen job and finding Pete, this was the best bit of luck I'd had in a long time. People say good things, same as bad ones, happen in threes so this was a prime example.

My new landlord and family were named Van Leiven. Father and head of the family, Emile Van

Leiven was a self-employed painter and decorator who ran his small business with just one partner and an apprentice. When business was not thriving very well during the war years, the family started taking in lodgers as the houses on their road were bigger than elsewhere in the neighbourhood, so they had extra space and this enabled them to make ends meet more easily. Madame Van Leiven was a plump, lively, motherly character who bustled round, making sure everyone in her family circle were comfortable and happy. The couple had five children. The eldest two were boy and girl twins, Laurence and Teresa. The others were girls – Maria, Elisabeth and Krysta. There would have been six but they lost one, a boy, through a tragic accident at home when, as a mischievous toddler, he fell into a wash boiler of hot suds and, consequently, was scalded to death. Madame Van Leiven blamed herself for a few years despite reassurances from family and friends that no housewife was expected to be superhuman. Any wife and mother had a tough job bringing up a young family so anyone could have a moment of inadvertence. There but for the grace of God any of us could experience a tragedy like this. Nevertheless, it was years before Lucie Van Leiven could talk about the accident to anyone outside their family.

Teresa was the one I was closest to and with whom I soon established a special relationship. She was a lively, bubbly youngster, outgoing, confident and extrovert like my late mother had been. She had the sort of nature to which shyness and self-consciousness were completely alien. Yet, her confidence in her contacts and dealings with people had absolutely nothing cheeky or arrogant about it. In spite of the twelve years difference in our ages we shared similar interests. I found myself wishing I had been like Teresa when I was growing up as shyness and some lack of self-confidence was often my problem as I adjusted to adult life. Although Teresa was only fourteen, she already competently looked after her two younger sisters, Elisabeth and Krysta, ably assisted by her next younger sister, Maria. Sometimes she had to guide and direct Maria as well because Maria was somewhat scatter-brained and impetuous. However, like Teresa, she had a likeable personality, being full of enthusiasm for life and good fun to be with. The girls' assistance was an invaluable help to Madame as she could now do a part-time job at one of the local stores for five mornings per week thus providing welcome supplementary income for herself and the family.

Teresa was almost as good as her mother in taking care of Elisabeth whose childhood was dogged with health problems. Elisabeth was born anaemic and wasn't expected to survive but inside her delicate, small body was a fighting spirit who won her battle for life against all the odds. Her special iron-rich and vitamin diet hadn't been easy to adhere to during wartime as, although we suffered less food shortages than other occupied countries, different food varieties were often difficult and occasionally impossible to obtain regularly so unbalanced diets were commonplace. Therefore,

Elisabeth's health needed extra building up so her mother was naturally relieved to have such a good nursing aide as Teresa at home.

While in Edegen, living with the Van Leivens, I heard some news about a somewhat dramatic development concerning my first boyfriend, Hendrik Varens, now deceased.

As I previously mentioned, he was killed in the Battle of Stalingrad. As he had fought for the Nazis, naturally his memory was not honoured by right-thinking people in Antwerp. In our small city, where so many of us knew each other, our news grapevine soon travelled fast through the neighbourhood. Madame Varens, my ex-boyfriend's mother received a shock one day when his wife, a young German woman turned up on her doorstep with her small son. It appeared that Hendrik had met, developed a romantic relationship with her and they married in Nazi Germany. Madame Varens now had a new daughter-in-law and grandson which she'd never even known existed! Understandably, at first she wasn't very pleased about this situation as, being originally Dutch, she knew only too well how much her own people had suffered under the Nazi occupation of her former country. However, being a compassionate person by nature and, soon discovering that her German daughter-in-law had come to her late husband's family for practical support and a settled home as she and her child were now homeless and destitute, having lost all her family in battles and Allied bombings, she took her in. Fortunately, it worked out better than anyone could have imagined, the girl and her little boy showed her gratitude in many ways and eventually became popular, well respected members of our community.

My romance with Pete really blossomed into a full scale affair. Looking back, I realise I was rather vulnerable, having just lost my mother, on not very good terms with my father, my relatives deeply wrapped up in their own concerns. Apart from my friends at the canteen and the Van Leivens I was alone in the world so my relationship with Pete was very welcome. We spent regular weekends together at the small apartment we rented between us and occasionally in my attic bedroom when the family were absent. The latter rendezvous has]d to be planned carefully as my friendly landlord or landlady could sometimes turn up unexpectedly. A bit of amorous intrigue only added more spice and fun.

On that note Marie ended their session. Bill and Harry cracked a couple of jokes and made comments that men often do about matters romantic with some sexual connotations. Mock disapproval and witty repartee were included. Their weekly meeting had become so routine that they could scarcely imagine any week without them. The very important purpose behind them made the friends all the more supportive of Marie in every way.

Chapter 24 – Love and Marriage

Marie's narrative continued as usual at their next meeting.

Apart from the fun, passion and romance in our relationship, I desperately wanted to be loved and give love in return. At long last it was happening. When Pete went on a 48 hour leave for a quick visit to England to see his Mum and younger brother who'd also been on active service in North Africa, taking part in the battle of El Alamein, I received two eloquent love letters from him. In them, he declared that even if I lived somewhere far distant like Canada or Australia he would move heaven on earth to reach me. To this day I've kept those letters as, despite the ups and downs in our marriage, at least here was someone prepared to give real love and genuine commitment. Letters like these are for all time a wonderful boost to any woman's self-esteem and morale especially if, like me, they'd been let down or had suffered bad treatment from men in the past. Even though they probably sounded, to a truly liberated female of our present time, like a hack imitation of a Mills & Boon paperback romance, in risky wartime situations, they possessed a rare poignancy.

"Yes, our later generations don't realise how lucky they are," Freda remarked, strong emotion in her voice. "Never knowing if their fiancés` or husbands were going to survive the war. It must have been a great relief to you that Pete wasn't in the infantry or a secret agent behind enemy lines."

"It certainly was!" Marie replied with equal fervour.

"Anyway, while Pete was on his short period of leave I discovered that I was pregnant, so three months later we were married. The British Army chaplain officiated. I wore a navy and white two-piece, purchased with ration coupons I'd saved. A bright red rose decorated one of the jacket lapels. Peter was looking very smart and handsome in his REME uniform. We stayed at my lodgings. Teresa was a godsend to us after our baby daughter, Sonia, was born. She helped me take care of her and loved taking her out in the antique but well- maintained pram provided by Madame Leiven. In those days of ingenious economy amongst ordinary working folk she'd kept it for the grandchildren, if and when they arrived. In any case, material goods were in short supply so I doubted if we could have bought anything superior. It more than likely would have been makeshift and not half as practical in design.

Sonia was a lovely baby with Pete's dark, wavy hair and slate blue-grey eyes. Everyone said she looked like every little girl's favourite doll. I thought somewhat humorously but with realism that she looked as though I'd had nothing to do with her conception and birth. She didn't even resemble my parents. However there was no doubt about her parentage on the paternal side. Her appearance made her instantly recognized as a Beresford. This period of my life from 1944-49 was certainly the most eventful and wonderful one ever.

It's often been said, and is very true, that you don't really get to know another person well unless you either live or work with them for a few years. For me, Pete epitomised the perfect young English gentleman but when I'd spent some weekends with him shortly before and after we were married, there were times when he exasperated me by his dawdling, poor time-keeping when we'd arranged an outing together or a social visit and his little Englander superiority air he used to put on when he criticized my people, their habits, culture and way of life. As to his first shortcoming, I wondered how he managed in the army, knowing what sticklers for time-keeping and punctuality they obviously needed to be.

"You can say that again!" Bill and harry chorused ruefully, having both served their terms of National Service in the 1950s.

"Oh by the way, Marie," Freda chimed in. "Hope you received this message too, Gloria. Our treasurer, Bob and your Joe are both very enthusiastic about

Marie's story. Bob wants to have it put on a flash drive which I think is a wonderful device. It stores oodles of documents, even full-length novels. This will be ideal for Marie's story."

Both Marie and Gloria were delighted with this latest development.

Marie then continued with her story.

"As I've just said, the army with their strict time-keeping must have been a tough challenge for Pete with his day-dreaming, absent-minded tendencies. However, one redeeming feature made up for this short coming in his personality – his considerable musical skills. He played tenor saxophone in the army's dance band, having learned this skill as a trainee musician before the war. On this subject, he often felt resentful at being conscripted into the army at the outbreak of war and maintained that, but for this he may well have succeeded in becoming a professional musician. When feeling sometimes fed up with everyday life he said indignantly that he'd had enough disadvantages as a poor widow's son, having to go out to work as soon as he was fourteen to earn a living and so contribute towards the humble finances of their little household instead of attending music college like sons from better off family backgrounds with BOTH parents could do. Instead Pete was apprenticed to train as a motor mechanic at a local garage. He'd just about served his time when he was called up for military service.

Although I never said so to him as I thought it would be rather tactless and unfeeling, I doubted very much if he'd ever have the determination and ambition to become a professional musician or the audacity to make his own luck by ensuring he "got the breaks in the right place at the right time" as they say in show business. Pete was never one to be adventurous or relish conflict and risk-taking and was really too gentlemanly to push himself forward when the occasion demanded. He was more of a plodder at work and a musical dabbler in his spare time.

It was interesting how the war was regarded by

some people as their curse and others as their salvation. I supposed it depended on each individual's circumstances. With his army experience working on their tanks and lorries proving to enhance his talent in this direction, Pete became a very good motor mechanic. This secured him a permanent job at his local MMB (Milk Marketing Board) depot. He was hard-working, conscientious and dedicated. Years later he received an award for being the longest serving employee at the depot. Pete did like living in Belgium, learned some Flemish, at least enough to get by in our community and generally got on well with my people. My late Mum would certainly have liked him. They'd have had a fair amount in common. Sometimes I felt a bit sad that she hadn't lived long enough to know him. He was tempted to stay in Belgium for good, but he was promised a job in England at one of his local garages. He'd also learned to drive while on army service. However, he felt under a moral obligation to return with our family to England as he promised to look after his widowed mother to whom he felt partially responsible, and also to repay, in some measure, for the way she'd loved, cared for and brought up him and his brother so well. Pete was only nine years old and his brother, Bernard, four and a half when their father died of heart failure brought on by rheumatic fever. I heartily agreed that she'd shown considerable courage and strength of character as a single parent under considerable pressure from relatives to send her boys to a childrens' home, in her determination to keep them and bring them up to be good, honest, kind and useful citizens, possessing integrity in plenty.

When this meeting ended, Marie addressed her small audience with this message:" Next time will be the final episode, as otherwise I'll end up going on forever with it and it'll be an impractical length for publication within a village fund-raising project. In a way it's a pity as my experiences in this country during the austerity period of the late 1940's and early 1950s were quite interesting, amusing, too, but I'll mention a few in my last chapter."

Chapter 25 – Final Episode

The friends gathered together at the club for the last part of Marie's story before the all-decisive committee meeting which would also involve the local councillors and news media. As usual, Marie delighted her audience with her interesting and lively story-telling.

"Before I left Belgium, I knew I'd one more matter to finally settle. Pete and I were married while he was still on active service so the ceremony was a civil one at the army head quarter's office. However we were not completely married as regards my church. As I was brought up a Roman Catholic and my husband was a Protestant – a Methodist what's more and, before the war, had been a keen member of Brook Lane Chapel at Alderley Edge, I would have had to leave my church and join Pete's denomination, or persuade Pete to join mine. The latter course of action was unlikely to succeed. I also knew that if I remained a Catholic it would be expected of me to bring up Sonia and any other children we might have, as Catholics. However I was, by now, pretty disillusioned with my branch of Christianity.

According to the Roman Catholic Church, I was a double sinner having given myself to Marc in all good faith, thinking at the time that doubtless we'd be married within a year and with Pete because at last I'd found someone whom I could trust not to let me down. I also loved him in spite of his faults and I'd learned to cope with his few shortcomings. The ideal of my church, as with Christian churches in general, was for a young couple to stay virgins until marriage. Indeed before the war I'd known of instances in my local church where some couples who were deeply in love, well-suited to each other, who married and were all set for a happy marriage lasting for life. However, I reflected, not everyone is as fortunate nor are their circumstances always as straightforward as this. My church would expect me to give up Pete and try to find someone else who would conform to their ideal. At best they'd expect me to marry Pete within a very short time because we'd had sex before marriage. As it happened, we did marry sooner than we'd planned because I discovered I was pregnant after we'd been going steady for nearly a year.

The war had also disrupted young adult life, in case the Catholic Church authorities hadn't noticed. If your fiance` was on active service in the infantry, the Marines or the RAF Bomber Command, it was a distinct possibility that he might get killed in action, so it was small wonder that couples snatched what ultimate happiness on the physical side of their relationship was available while on a short-term of leave which could often be only 48 hours. In occupied countries such as mine had been, some girls' steady boyfriends were in The Resistance or were Allied secret agents so the danger of death or capture by the enemy, resulting in certain death, this fear was every bit as prevalent as within the armed forces. Couples who truly loved each other and so were fully committed in their relationship, I reflected, wouldn't turn unfaithful or promiscuous anyway. I'd also thought for a long time that, unlike other church denomination's counselors, you could hardly ask for guidance on contraceptives, family planning or advice on sex problems in marriage should they occur, from a nun or a priest. Looking at this area of Christian teaching of which I'd always been reluctant to be overly judgmental, I still admired couples who stuck to the Christian way of lifelong love and commitment in their marriages. Of course, most of my generation found this easier as we weren't having to contend with difficult moral dilemmas and confusion plus emotional insecurity caused by the permissive society in the following decades but one.

"Yes, Marie it certainly put my daughter in an awkward, unenviable position after being divorced from her first husband," said Doreen ruefully. "She had to be very wary for the sake of her schoolboy son and herself that she didn't let someone over her threshold who was only after sex once they'd enjoyed couple of romantic nights out."

"It seems from what you'd explained to me about her before when we met for a coffee and chat at the news café` in town, she did very well to adhere to her principles," replied Marie. "Anyway I'm so pleased she found happiness with Jack, the second-time round. To return to my story: my disillusionment with my church was triumphant, so when settled in England I changed over to Protestantism and either attended the local Anglican church or the Methodist one. This is likely to be the same policy for the rest of my life. Anyhow, having been married in a secular setting, presided over by the army chaplain and registered in the forces' files, Pete and I later received a blessing and renewal of our vows at our local Anglican Parish Church."

Marie and friends then took a short break for afternoon tea refreshments. They returned to being an audience for Marie's final narrative.

"After bidding a most emotional farewell to the

Van Leiven family and promising to keep in touch, we finally left with Sonia for England in January 1947. Apart from a couple of short holidays in Belgium during 1949 and 1951, on both occasions to visit the Van Leivens, I severed my connection with my native land without regret. (Apart from that appalling winter of 1947 when I needed true British grit and Dunkirk spirit to endure it and emerge unscathed!) I looked forward to making a fresh start in the country I'd now adopted as my own and was determined to do all in my power to be a really good wife and mother. Last but not least, a loyal, enthusiastic British citizen.

For me, at first this was quite a challenge as England was a grey, spartan and utilitarian place where "mend and make do" was still prevalent as the country recovered from the war. Nearby Manchester, in common with several other industrial cities, still had visible bomb damage and buildings were blackened by over a century of industrial pollution. I remember trying to concoct something like an occasional more imaginative meal out of the government's quota of family weekly rations. There wasn't much variety of food in the shops at that time so Pete was delighted when I used some imagination in cooking so he didn't have to put up with the same old dull culinary fare week after week. My considerable experience as head cook and housekeeper back in Belgium was useful in more ways than the obvious one.

My family and I were lucky in that Pete's mother, Nellie lived in a little terraced cottage in the countryside, down a leafy lane called Brook Lane, about a mile from the centre of Alderley village. We lived with Nellie here until 1952, after which we moved into our permanent home, a council house on the new estate, closer to the village centre. (These houses were promised to ex-military service personnel for after the war had ended.) Nellie's cottage was a super home where we spent five and a half happy years. It had a small, pretty garden and open fields just beyond. It was especially wonderful in springtime when the field became a sea of frothy pink and white ladies' smock, golden daffodils, snowdrops and mauve-coloured wild crocuses. The garden, too, was a riot of colour when the spring and summer flowers bloomed. Despite having no electricity, just gas lights and oil lamps upstairs, an outside toilet and an antique radio which Nellie had purchased from a second-hand sale room but which nevertheless had very good sound quality for its age, we were not discontented. Even with a lack of some material benefits, we were more than compensated by a happy relaxed atmosphere, a friendly neighbourhood that possessed good community spirit, and the fun of making our own entertainment. (apart from a few nights out at shows by our local amateur dramatic and operatic societies at the village hall and a small cinema). Nellie also ran a small holding in a corner of the back garden, keeping chickens, so we always had a plentiful supply of fresh eggs.

Both of us were very sorry to leave when our new home was ready for us to move in, but this had to be because of insufficient room for Sonia's possessions now she was bigger and I was expecting our second child, due in January 1953. We had a son, so our family was now complete. To cut a longer story short, I feel I've been privileged in having raised two good children who've grown up to be basically kind, helpful and public-spirited which I value much more than these high fliers, obsessed with making money and material success, nearly burning themselves out to become millionaires before they reach their mid-thirties."

After applause, Marie announced that she'd give a short speech at Torr Brookdale's Community Centre AGM to conclude her long narrative and thank the club members for their support and Gloria informed the group that the completed book would be presented to the committee at this same meeting, as they all departed for home.

Final Outcome and Epilogue

At the all-important meeting which they all attended, Marie made a short speech to thank her supporters at the club. By her short final speech, she hoped to influence the committee even more as regards her fund-raising contribution for the centre.

"On a personal note, I now have four grandchildren of which I'm also very proud. My husband, Pete, fortunately lived long enough to enjoy, help and guide them when growing up. He was a friend, lover and loyal supporter until his death from heart failure three years ago, so I consider myself to be most fortunate to have experienced such a good marriage. Particularly for my daughter, Sonia and son-in-law, Martin, life had not been easy as their son exhibited behaviour problems, both at home and in school. Finally, when a teenager, he was diagnosed with Asperger's Syndrome, so it was such a relief to receive the practical support he so desperately needed. It's taken many years but he's independent now, lives in a shared house and even has a job as a kitchen porter in a large local restaurant. My other grandchildren have also overcome problems which included temporary hearing difficulties, sports injuries and lack of self-confidence but are now doing well at college. One out of the three has completed her college course, gained her qualifications and is now employed as support worker for children with learning difficulties. This has spurred me on, making me determined to see my project through because of all the potential good it will achieve both for our centre and our wider community. Many thanks to all my friends here at the centre for being such patient, good listeners throughout my long narrative as well as your interesting comments you so willingly contributed."

After much enthusiastic applause the launch and sales of Marie's book, as part of ongoing fund-raising efforts to secure a National Lottery grant for the centre's future, was discussed. The committee had a battle to fight to convince two skeptical members, Beryl Greenfield, centre secretary and Martin Williamson, centre manager that Marie's book would be a significant, fund-raising enterprise to add to the money already raised towards their grant application.

"There's so many of these "the way we were/memory lane" sort of paperback literature about these days not to mention Amazon offering them in e-book form online," Martin argued. "What makes this one any different or superior?"

Robert Silverstone, club treasurer, disagreed. "This one has a continental slant on a familiar modern history period, so a different point of view from our British perspective is expressed which always adds some originality. Marie and her friends have worked very hard to produce this book which will also be of local interest anyway. I vote that we accept the book launch and sales venture as I believe it could be most successful."

As the rest of the committee backed Robert's

opinion on the matter, the publication, launch and book signing sales event all went ahead. Extra publicity resulted in Marie, the friends, Gloria and her husband, Joe, and the rest of the club committee having this news and their photos featured in both local and regional newspapers. Their group photo even appeared in the County Council's quarterly magazine. Marie's book also received a favourable review by a leading journalist and literary critic in the regional newspaper, echoed by his local counterpart.

As the book proved to be a runaway success as regards sales, the chances of the lottery bid being equally successful were much improved.

"Certainly a whole lot more than I or any of us thought possible from an old lady's reminiscences of her life experiences," Marie beamed.

"Oh, you'd be surprised," Gloria and Joe chipped in. "People are often looking for something that is a bit different to read. Anyway, this certainly calls for a celebration. Our Robert, the treasurer, is full of surprises, too. He's booked us in for a posh special dinner at the Old Roebuck Inn. I vote we give him a present on the night for all his loyalty and encouragement throughout this project."

The friends' circle all readily agreed to this suggestion. Bill added: "Reverend Norman also managed to twist the arm of a major North West charitable trust, secured financial support from that computer firm down on Swallows Beck Industrial Estate, so the National Lottery fund couldn't bypass us easily now that we've got all this financial backing for our bid!"

"There's going to be a double celebration at the Roebuck, friends," Harry and Rosemary chorused, both looking extremely happy. "We've decided to tie the knot and invite you to our wedding in seven months' time!"

Acknowledgements

My Late Parents' Memories without which this book would not have materialized.

John Edmunds, active member of New Mills Revival Church who assisted me in the early stages of this publication.

Pastor Sam Fentem, Old Trafford Pentecostal Church who gladly gave me help and advice with this book's production.

Tom Taylor, Manager of Café Revive, New Mills and his friend, Sylvia Wright who kindly proof read my book for me.

Peter Beardwood, computer specialist at the CVS (Commission for Voluntary Services in High Peak who kindly checked over and formatted this book
The friendly and helpful staff of Stockport Central Library

Belgium – A History by Bernard A Cook. Google Books

Wikipedia the Free Encyclopedia

www.historvius.com/worldwar1

The Belgian Air Force in the First world War by Walter Pieters – published by Peter Lang.

Website: www.belgian-wings/worldwar1aviation

Political History of Belgium from 1830 onwards by ELS Witte, Google Books.

Belgium in World War 2 - The German Occupation, Wikipedia Books on World War 2.

Battle for Antwerp – The Liberation of a City by J L Moulton, Book Club Associates, London.

Liberation of Belgium 1944. www.veterans.gc.ca Canadian_Armed Forces in the Two World Wars website.

Useful information snippets from *Eye Witness Travel* published by Dorling Kindersley, London – main contributor, Antony Mason and Belgium & Luxemburg guidebook published by Lonely Planet, originators,

Tony & Maureen Wheeler, contributory writers, M Elliott and H Smith.